The 1840s gothic tales by Khoma Kupriyenko

the
Evil
Prophet

sova
BOOKS

First edition

Copyright © 2024 by Sova Books Pty Ltd

ISBN: 978-0-6489485-7-5

Translation: Svitlana Chornomorets
                    Lesia Andriyashyk
        Design: Andrii Kharlov

The 1840s gothic tales by

Khoma Kupriyenko

The Evil Prophet

2024

Contents

Listening to what my friend was saying, at first, I got scared because he was right when he said, "They will mock you endlessly." But then I thought it over that I am not writing to be praised or criticised; no! Not at all! I want people to know what I have written—because there is a lot of truth here, and maybe not everyone has heard about what I have shared in my book.

And if people criticise me and want to mock me, well, so be it! This is just my first attempt at writing, and I didn't manage to put everything together perfectly—I did it the best I could! Even if they laugh at me, I still won't stop writing, and I'll soon finish my second book. Say what you will about me.

Khoma Kupriyenko

Introduction

The two novellas and two short stories presented here were originally published as a collection entitled *Ukrainian Novellas and Stories by Khoma Kupriyenko*[1], in 1840. Notably, this was the same year that Taras Shevchenko's iconic Kobzar was first published. However, Kupriyenko's publication was notably omitted from Komarov's *Bibliographic Index*[2]. This omission is striking, considering that, according to the *Bibliographic Index*, only forty Ukrainian titles were published between 1798 and 1840—less than one book per year. As Volodymyr Danylov[3] noted in his article, the forty-first book in the Ukrainian language, regardless of its literary merit, would have been a noteworthy contribution.

Despite promising to release a second volume, Kupriyenko's plans were never realised, possibly due to the hostile reception from literary critics at the time. Indeed, Kupriyenko's book went rather unnoticed except for a few negative reviews by Russian literary critics.[4][5] Interestingly, Kupriyenko predicted a poor reception of his book. In his preface, he reproduced his dialogue with his friend, where the latter tried to convince the author to keep his work to himself and to share it perhaps only in the company of friends.

While his stories may lack the emotional depth or detailed descriptions of nature found in more celebrated works, they offer a unique glimpse into a storytelling style closely resembling modern urban legends.

Also, despite their simplicity, these tales are valuable for understanding the Ukrainian folklore of the era. Perhaps for that reason, Khoma Kupriyenko dedicated his book to Hrytsko Osnovyanenko (Hryhoriy Kvitka-Osnovyanenko; 1778–1843), a prominent Ukrainian writer, playwright, and cultural figure widely regarded as one of the founders of modern Ukrainian literature. Osnovyanenko's works often drew upon the rich folklore, oral traditions, and cultural practices of the Ukrainian people. It is likely that Osnovyanenko, rather than Mykola Hohol (Nikolai Gogol), as some believe, was the primary influence on Kupriyenko's folklore-saturated novellas.

In his preface, Kupriyenko emphasised the ethnographic value of his stories, stating: "I want people to know what I have written because there is a lot of truth here, and perhaps not everyone has heard about what I have told in my book". By "truth", he was likely referring to the real legends and beliefs that were part of the everyday life of the people.

There is no information available about who Khoma Kupriyenko was. No documents or personal memoirs mention this name, leaving us without direct details about his life. However, Volodymyr Danilov[6], through an analysis of Kupriyenko's writing style, orthography, and vocabulary, has drawn some intriguing conclusions.

Danilov believes that Khoma Kupriyenko likely hailed from the Chernihiv region in Northern Ukraine. He supports this theory, in part, by referencing a legend from Chernihiv about a dead warlock returning to life, a story echoed in Kupriyenko's work. Danilov's analysis also suggests that Kupriyenko may have been a young seminary student, potentially following in the footsteps of Hryhoriy Kvitka-Osnovyanenko and Mykola Hohol.

Svitlana Chornomorets
August, 2024

Endnotes

[1] Kupriyenko K., 1840, *Malorossiyskie povesti i rasskazy Khomy Kupriyenko* [Ukrainian Novellas and Stories by Khoma Kupriyenko], Moscow, The Lazarev Institute of Oriental Languages Press.

[2] Komarov, M., 1883, *Bibliografichnyi Pokazhchyk Novoi Ukrainskoi Literatury: (1798-1883)* [Bibliographic Index of New Ukrainian Literature: (1798-1883)], Kyiv, H. T. Korchak-Novytskyi Press.

[3] Danilov, V., 1928, "Ukrainskie rasskazy Kupriyenko, 1840 hoda" [Ukrainian short stories by Kupriyenko, 1840], *Yuvileynyi Zbirnyk na Poshanu Akademyka Mykhaila Serhiyovycha Hrushevskoho* [Jubilee Collection in Honor of Academician Mykhailo Serhiyovych Hrushevsky], Kyiv, Ukrainska Akademiya Nauk [The National Academy of Sciences of Ukraine], vol. 2, pp. 64-71.

[4] Unknown, 1840, "Malorossiyskie povesti i rasskazy Khomy Kupriyenko" [Little Russian (Ukrainian) novellas and short stories by Khoma Kupriyenko], in "Bibliograficheskaya khronika" [Bibliographic chronicle], *Otechestvennyia Zapiski* [Fatherland Notes], vol. 10, pp. 24-25.

[5] Unknown, 1840, "Malorossiyskie rasskazy Khomy Kupriyenko" [Little Russian (Ukrainian) short stories by Khoma Kupriyenko], in "Literaturnaya letopis" [Literary chronicle], *Biblioteka dlia Chteniya* [Library for Reading], vol. 40, pp. 1-2.

[6] Danilov, V., 1928, *abid.*

The Evil Prophet

Chapter One
"The Cuckoo's Call"

He who has never ventured into the village of K... has indeed missed a marvel!

"What sort of village could it be?" you might wonder, dear readers.

It is indeed a great village, take it from me: one could say it boasts close to a thousand residents. Yet, it's not the number of residents that's remarkable... What I must tell you is that there are so many witches in this village, it seems to me, there are more here than in the entire wide world, causing an incredible amount of trouble for the poor inhabitants!.. The tales told to me by the people of this village made my hair stand on end. So, if you will, dear readers, allow me to share what I've heard from the residents of this village. Listen well! But please, kindly refrain from being upset if my narration appears somewhat convoluted...

In this very village, close to the church, at the very spot where now lives the blacksmith Pankratenko, there once was the dwelling of the church elder, Okhrym Prokopenko, a man of considerable wealth. And why wouldn't he be? After all, he held the position of elder.

His livestock were numerous: around twenty-five horses, three pairs of oxen, and even a flock of sheep. He owned chickens, geese, and even turkeys; as for his fields, their expanse was vast – its true extent known to few. With the arrival of spring, villagers would queue at his door, each with a plea:

"Uncle, dear! Might you lend us a bit of your land to till? We'd be forever in your debt. Come summer, when

it's time to harvest or mow, we'll ensure you're amply rewarded."

Okhrym, true to his nature, never turned anyone away and generously lent his land to all who asked. His reputation for benevolence spread far and wide, and the villagers held him in high esteem, men tipping their hats to him upon crossing paths.

Whenever the judge made rounds to the village, his stay would invariably be at Okhrym's residence. Should the need arise for something as simple as hot water from a samovar, Okhrym would invite him over and cater to his needs. And in gratitude for this, when holidays approached and the judge visited the village, he would slip Okhrym a hundred rubles as a gift. To Okhrym, a hundred rubles was but a trifle! Yet, this gesture earned him the privilege to converse with the judge as though he were his brother, even sharing a bench as equals.

He had a wife named Vivdia and a daughter, Oksenia. His daughter was strikingly beautiful, truly exceptional in appearance. When she strolled down the street, young men would flock to her, stubbornly refusing to leave.

Should any suitor try to woo her, she would immediately blush and respond, "Go away! Leave me alone! You have your own beloved. I neither have nor desire one!"

They would then leave her alone, shifting their attention to another girl. Oksenia, after staying for a while longer, would head home and begin bustling about the house. She was incredibly industrious, and barely took a moment to sit down, always engrossed in her chores.

At seventeen, Oksenia had many admirers, yet none appeared suitable to her. Her father and mother respected her wishes and did not pressure her to marry someone of their choosing, but not hers.

But could it truly be said that she had no sweetheart? For a girl of seventeen, such a notion seemed far-fetched! Indeed, the truth was... She loved Ivan Nastenko, the son of the *otaman*. It must be acknowledged; they were an admirable match. Ivan, a handsome youth, and Oksenia, a beautiful young woman. Their encounters on the street drew admiring glances, with onlookers remarking, "What a splendid pair they are! With God's blessing, a wedding shall soon be upon us, and I shall revel, toasting to the health of the bride and groom!"

How their love story began – I cannot say for certain, but I will share with you what I've heard, dear readers, to the best of my ability. On Saturday, the eve of *Klechalna Sunday*, Ivan and Oksenia decided to meet at night in the orchard belonging to Oksenia's father for a private conversation. And so, they followed through with their plan. After supper at home, Ivan slipped into a white *svyta*, fastened a red belt around his waist, donned his hat, and set out. He arrived at the designated spot in the orchard where Oksenia had promised to meet him, took a seat under a tree, and waited for her. Before long, Oksenia appeared, and upon seeing Ivan, she ran to embrace him, showering him with kisses and exclaiming, "Hello, my sweetheart, my falcon!"

And he, embracing her, replied, "Hello, my little bird, my Oksenia! II long for autumn to arrive so we can marry and find peace, but something weighs heavily on my heart, and I've been plagued by horrid nightmares. Last night I

had a dream too horrible to tell. It seemed to me that we were being separated; and guess by whom, my dove..." In that instant, Ivan made the sign of the cross, "I envisioned us in the forest, and as dusk approached, we were making our way home, taking the main road into the city. We walked, arm in arm, but suddenly, as if out of nowhere, my aunt Stepanyda, Redka's wife, appeared. She rushed over, seized you in her embrace, and disappeared into the ground. That's when I awoke."

"Indeed," Oksenia said, "this dream portends something ominous. And what's worst is that your aunt appeared in it – people say she's the most powerful witch, God forbid! You've mentioned she bore ill will towards your father, Ivan, something wicked is bound to happen."

"This is true," Ivan said. "When I asked my father why he didn't get along with my aunt and never invited her over, he simply replied, 'To hell with her! She mingles with unclean spirits!' "

No sooner had Ivan spoken than something rustled the leaves nearby. They looked to see a huge pig, as large as a cow, storming past them like a whirlwind. Ivan and Oksenia were petrified. They crossed themselves and were just about to rush home when they heard another rustling behind them. They turned around – a woman in a white *sorochka* was charging towards them. They were rooted to the spot in fear. She approached and spoke:

"Here you are, Ivan, alongside your beloved, dreaming she will become your wife. Your father deeply offended me. I will bring misfortune upon you, for I have already sworn revenge on your family. Farewell!" With these words, she unleashed a laugh so chilling that Ivan and Oksenia felt a shiver cascade down their spines.

Ivan and Oksenia sat frozen beneath the tree. They could not comprehend what was happening before them. Gradually, Ivan mustered some courage, made the sign of the cross, and said:

"The Holy Mother of God protects us! What malevolent force has cast its shadow over us? Arise, Oksenia, we must hasten home."

Oksenia stood up, crossed herself, and said, "Let's go, my dear Ivan. Let's go!"

Ivan, though trembling as if from a severe winter chill, still embraced Oksenia and hurried with her to escape from that cursed orchard. Oksenia's house was not far, and when she reached her yard, she bid farewell to Ivan. She did not want to part with him, but she had to. Inside the house, the lights remained lit because a major holiday[1] was approaching, and everyone was preparing.

"It seems, old woman," said Oksenia's father, settling in and undressing to go to bed, "that our Oksenia is taking her time at her aunt's."

15

Oksenia had told her parents that she was visiting her aunt to borrow a necklace for the forthcoming feast day. Despite possessing an array of necklaces, some quite lavish, she insisted she needed something different for the occasion – ah, vanity of a maiden! Indeed, her true intent was to slip away to the orchard.

"She might be staying over for the night," suggested Oksenia's mother.

No sooner had she said that when – the door creaked – and Oksenia, white as a sheet, rushed into the house, swiftly taking a seat on the bench. Both the father and the mother were frightened to see their daughter so pale and bursting into the house without saying a word.

"Something must have scared her," they thought.

"God be with you, daughter!" they exclaimed. "Why are you so pale? Did something wicked frighten you."

Gradually regaining her composure, Oksenia began to tell them that indeed something happened as she was returning from her aunt's, albeit she omitted that it had taken place in their very orchard.

"...I was just nearing our orchard when a huge pig emerged and dashed past me so closely I feared it might topple me. And then," Oksenia went on, "I glanced back – oh, by the Lord's grace! – the pig disappeared as if into thin air. In its place, I saw a woman in a white *sorochka* hurrying down the street, and I rushed into our yard."

The father and mother were astonished by what their daughter was telling them, and then they began to fuss and worry around her to make sure that nothing had really happened to her from the scare she endured.[2]

Reflecting on the peculiar incident, the family extinguished the lamp and retired for the night. Yet, before sleep could claim them, an unusual event unfolded. They heard a cuckoo calling from a tree right next to the window that faced the orchard. It is well known that if a cuckoo starts calling at night, it is considered an ill omen. It definitely foretells something bad, such as significant loss or a death in the household it chooses to call. The old man considered to himself that her call was an ominous sign and that they were unlikely to avoid a troublesome hour. Then, with a deep sigh, he fell into a profound sleep.

Yet Oksenia spent the entire night awake and heard the cursed cuckoo call out until the very dawn. Just before daylight, she barely closed her eyes, only to find no peace even then – terrible dreams haunted her. It seemed to her that the cursed witch stood at the window, where the cuckoo had been calling, staring relentlessly at her, her eyes glowing like embers and teeth gnashing.

Then it seemed to her that she and Ivan were together in the orchard, at the very spot where they had met the evening before, and suddenly, out of nowhere, the witch appeared and began to scold them, repeating the same words: "I shall bring misfortune upon you, Ivan!" and then let out a loud laugh and disappeared from their sight.

Oksenia had slept for a long time; the sun was already high, and her mother had heated the house, but she was still dreaming. When she woke up, she told them about her dream. Both her father and mother were astonished, especially when they heard about the cuckoo.

"Well," the old man said, "you cannot escape the wrath of God – may His holy will be done! Surely the cuckoo foretold something bad."

The old man crossed himself, and tears fell from his eyes. Seeing this, his daughter and wife also crossed themselves and wept bitterly.

"Don't cry," the old man said. "Hopefully, God will have mercy on us."

✳✳✳

Now let's see what our Ivan was doing. Just after he said goodbye to Oksenia and hadn't yet walked half the way, out of nowhere a white ball the size of a large head rolled under his feet[3]. Poor Ivan lost his balance and crashed to the ground with full force.

"What in the world!" Ivan thought, then he got up, made the sign of the cross, looked around, but there was nothing: the ball had vanished. Ivan hurried towards home. He had not gone more than ten steps when he glanced back – there was a woman in a white *sorochka* following him, identical to the one he had seen in the orchard.

Ivan was terrified and, without looking back, ran with all his might towards home. He could not comprehend what was happening; he only felt that someone was chasing him. He finally reached his yard, and as soon as he jumped inside, he looked back – there stood the apparition by the gate, probably scared off by the dogs, which had howled loudly and quickly hid in the shed. The apparition shouted at him, "You won't escape my grasp!"

At this, Ivan was even more frightened and started banging desperately on the door – for it was locked and there was no light in the house. Ivan did not wait at the door for long; his mother soon came out and opened it for him.

"Where in the devil's name have you been wandering until midnight?" Ivan's mother chided him.

"Be quiet, Mom!" Ivan said, and quickly went inside the house, only to be confronted by his father, who also began scolding him for being so late.

"Be silent, don't scold, father! I barely escaped with my life." Ivan then began to tell his father and mother everything he had seen and what his Aunt Stepanyda had said to him in the orchard of church elder Okhrym Prokopenko. In his fright, Ivan confessed everything to his father and mother: that he had been there with Oksenia.

Upon hearing this, his father erupted, "And why, you foolish boy, would you choose to court a young woman just before such a significant holiday[4]? Couldn't you have picked a different time? Perhaps, indeed, God has permitted this cursed witch, my own sister, to cast misfortune upon you."

"Why did she say she was angry with you, father?" Ivan inquired.

"Why?" his father responded, "Well, here's the reason: She is undoubtedly a witch, and witches are known to sneak into people's barns to steal milk from their cows. Roughly five years ago, she intended to do just that to us. Every morning, when your mother would attempt to milk, not a single drop of milk would come out, only blood from the udders. Your mother told me about this; and I suspected that some witch was meddling with us.

***

" 'You just wait, you devil's kin,' I thought. 'I'll teach you a lesson for causing harm.' So, as night came, I put on my *svyta*, carved an aspen stake, went to the barn, and, hiding behind a harrow, sat in a corner.

I already knew how to do it – I had heard from the

old folks that a witch can only be hit with an aspen stake, and she won't detect your presence if you hide behind a harrow.[5]

So there I sat, waiting for her to come. I didn't have to wait long before I saw a woman in a white *sorochka*, with a milking pail on her head and her hair loose. At first, I was scared, but then I thought, 'I'm still young, strong, and I have a good stake...' As soon as she started milking the cows, I sprang from behind the harrow and struck her on the shoulders with all my might, once, and then a second, third time... My God!

She let the pail fall and commenced her pleas, whimpering for mercy: 'Spare me, good man, shall never repeat this deed, not in my lifetime, nor until the Day of Judgement! Please, release me! Do not strike again!..' "

But I didn't stop and kept beating her until, worn out, I seized her by the hair, hauled her out of the barn, and was about to demand her name when – to my shock – it was my cousin Stepanyda!

"What do you think you are doing?" I yelled at her. "I'll tie you up with ropes and tomorrow take you to court as soon as dawn breaks!"

She started wailing, "Forgive me, my brother, don't take me to court. You've already broken all my ribs!"

Well, as it was, I couldn't help but feel sorry for my

21

own kin. I let her go, warning her never to show her face in my yard again. I forgot, though, to make her swear not to perform any more witchcraft...

"Well, she has never returned to milk our cows again and we had plenty of milk. However, every single day in the village someone would complain that a witch had visited their yard.

"See, that's what I did to your aunt," Ivan's father said to his son, who listened in amazement. "Perhaps that's why she swore to take revenge on us. Perhaps God won't let the witch triumph over us, yet what troubles me is your timing in courting a young woman. Perhaps that will be the reason why God would punish us. Go to sleep, and don't ever do this again."

Having said that, Ivan's father crossed himself three times, lay down beside his wife, who had long since fallen asleep and hadn't heard her husband's story; and Ivan, after undressing, prayed to God and climbed onto the *pich*. He was unable to shake off his thoughts about his aunt and fear kept its grip on him, even though he was inside the house.

As soon as they extinguished the light, just like in Oksenia's case, a cuckoo appeared out of nowhere. It perched by the window and began to call.

"It foretells something wicked," Ivan's father sighed, then fell aslccp, snoring."

Ivan, much like Oksenia, remained awake through the night, haunted by the cuckoo's calls.

Only as dawn approached did he finally fell asleep and dreamed the same dream as Oksenia...

Chapter Two
"Autumn, Season of Weddings"

Autumn had come: all the villagers had completed their harvest and, after planting their crops, were now praying to the merciful God for a bountiful yield. It was a season when the elderly could finally rest from their summer toils and the youth celebrated their weddings.

This time, long anticipated, had subtly arrived.

In the households of Prokopenko and Nastenko, thoughts were solely on the upcoming wedding.

"You, Ivan," his father instructed, "will head to the market on Friday to purchase items needed for the wedding. On Saturday, we'll send the starosty to the bride's family."

Just then, they heard the church bell tolling.

"Why are they tolling?" Ivan's father wondered.

"Today is Monday and there's no holiday – I was in the village this morning and spoke with our deacon, Naum. He confirmed there's no holiday tomorrow either... Maybe it's for someone who has passed. Well, may they find eternal peace." Okhrym began to make the sign of the cross...

Just then, the tavern keeper, Perepelykha, entered the house. You see, she had heard that they were planning a wedding and wanted to suggest that they should buy *horilka* only from her.

"Good health to you!" Perepelykha greeted as she stepped inside. "I've heard from good people that you're planning your son's wedding – may God assist you in all your preparations! I've come to ask if you might need

horilka? Please consider buying it from me. I have excellent horilka, freshly brought from Vinnytsia just the other day."

"We thank you," Ivan's parents said together. "Please, have a seat."

"Did you hear," old Nastenko asked Perepelykha, "about anyone who died in our village? You must have heard something – people from all over the village come to you every day."

"Holy Fathers!" exclaimed Perepelykha, "I completely forgot to tell you, your relative Stepanyda has passed away. And, may God have mercy, she died a horrible death[6]! A woman who witnessed it was at my tavern this morning and told me everything. It was such a dreadful event!"

"And how did she die?" they all wondered.

"How?" Perepelykha replied, "This woman was there until the very end and told me everything. Just before she died, Stepanyda, with a voice not her own, screamed: 'Oh, poor me! Save my soul! Let me die! Oh, my heart aches! And who are you, standing at my head and feet? Did you come for my soul? Take it, but ensure I'm warm in your hell. Ah! I'm suffocating! It's so hot!' Then she looked at the people and cried: 'Good people! Save me!'

Everyone immediately realised that she was a witch. And when a witch dies, a part of her ceiling must be removed, otherwise she cannot pass away. There were elders there who knew this, and they quickly tore down the ceiling. As soon as they did, Stepanyda began to die: she closed her eyes, then opened them again, let out a loud laugh, and drew her last breath."

"May God punish this wicked kin," old Nastenko said, crossing himself. "She will answer for her deeds in the afterlife."

Perepelykha did not linger and soon left, intending to also visit the church elder to promote her *horilka* and secure a deal.

On the third day, Wednesday, the cursed witch was buried without a priest's involvement – since she was a witch, the priest refused to conduct her burial. Among themselves, the villagers continually referred to her as a witch and expressed relief at her death, blaming her for the many misfortunes that had plagued the village.

So, let the good people speculate as they wish, but we'll return to story of Ivan's and Oksenia's wedding.

Thursday came. The previous evening, Ivan's parents had discussed what they needed to buy at the market for their son's wedding.

Ivan went to bed early so he could rise at dawn the next day, because although the town was not too far, it was still about ten versts away.

Whether he slept long or not, suddenly he heard his

father waking him: "Rise, Ivan! Time to head to the market: it must be dawning soon."

Ivan got up, washed, said his prayers devoutly, dressed neatly, grabbed fifteen rubles, and departed. The night was dark and a bit chilly – a frost had set in.

Ivan walked briskly, thinking how fortunate he was to soon become Oksenia's husband.

Before long, Ivan walked past the village and came upon the cemetery, which lay just outside the village, near the main road. For some unknown reason, he felt a sense of sadness, especially when he passed by his aunt's grave.

Ivan made the sign of the cross and pressed forward. Reaching the main road, a spine-tingling fear overcame him, his hair stood on end. He felt as though someone was following him; he looked back... and, by the Lord's decree! At the cemetery, something as white as snow oscillated gently on a grave cross, sending shivers down Ivan's spine.

Seeing this, Ivan thought, "What am I to do?" and crossed himself again. "That's the end of me! I must run. But where to? I can't turn back – the white ghost is right by the very road. I'll run forward," Ivan thought. "Maybe I'll meet people going to the market."

He risked a glance back, and the apparition was close, surging straight toward him.

"What should I do now? Lord, have mercy! What

have I done to deserve this? I am surely lost!" Ivan thought as he began to sprint, barely feeling the ground beneath his feet.

Looking back again, he saw that a revenant was pursuing him and was almost upon him. Spotting a tree off the road, Ivan dashed towards it, thinking he could conceal himself there from the revenant. When he reached the tree, he found it was a willow, likely split by lightning, with a hollowed centre. He squeezed inside, crouched down, and shut his eyes, hoping to hide from the terrifying sight of the revenant.

Ivan was drenched in a cold sweat. Just when he thought he might be safe, he felt a nudge. He opened his

eyes and saw the revenant barely ten steps away, advancing closer... and closer...

"Here you are!" the revenant bellowed with a force that could have echoed across ten versts.

***

"Wake up, old woman!" Okhrym Prokopenko, Oksenia's father, said as he awoke. "And blow out the candles."

"Father, don't wake mother," Oksenia interjected, "I'll take care of it." She had been awake for hours, her thoughts consumed by Ivan.

As daylight seeped into the Prokopenko household, everyone arose to begin their day. Oksenia sat on the floor, peeling beetroots for *borshch*.

"Ha! Ha! Ha!.." An eerie laughter echoed outside the window of the Prokopenko home, so chilling that it turned the church elder and his wife pale.

"What was that laughter?" Okhrym exclaimed, making the sign of the cross as he peered toward the window – the latch was open. A hand, a shade of blue, reached inside, pointing directly at the floor where Oksenia lay hidden under a blanket. Startled by the laughter, she had thrown herself to the floor and covered herself in a bid to conceal her presence.

Okhrym and his wife stood petrified at the sight of the blue hand.

"Cock-a-doodle-do!"[7] a rooster crowed, and the hand vanished into thin air.

Both of them made the sign of the cross, feeling a bit relieved and less frightened.

"It's good that our Oksenia was asleep and didn't witness this apparition; it would have terrified her," remarked Oksenia's mother.

"Let her sleep in peace," old Prokopenko agreed.

As the dawn broke, the old woman kindled the fire in the house, but Oksenia remained asleep.

"Wake Oksenia up," the mother instructed her

husband as she stepped outside.

Okhrym got up from the bench where he had been sitting, walked over to the spot where his daughter was lying, and gently began to rouse her.

"Wake up, sweetheart!" he urged. "It's getting late – the morning is nearly gone!" In doing so, he accidentally touched her hand.

"Why are her hands so cold?" Okhrym wondered; he attempted to wake her again, but she did not respond. He slowly pulled back the blanket, only to find her entire body cold... He leaned down to listen – there was no breath.

"Oh, my God!" Okhrym cried out in despair, loud enough for his wife, who was in the yard feeding the pigs, to hear and rush into the house.

"What's happened?" asked Okhrym's wife.

"Oh, woe is us! Wife, look at Oksenia! She has died!"

Oksenia's mother was stunned.

"Oh, my God!" she wailed in deep sorrow. "My darling daughter, my dove! You were to be wed, but now you'll rest in the damp earth!"

"Good day!" Chehylo's son greeted as he burst into the house, only to see everyone crying as if mourning a death. Then he saw Oksenia lying lifeless on the floor. He was taken aback, having just seen her fetching water the previous day. Here they told him everything that had happened, and that someone had been reaching a blue hand through their window

"What a wicked occurrence!" the young man exclaimed. "And out there, near the village, close to the main road, they found a torn-apart man. Some *chumaky* were spending the night nearby, and they said they heard someone scream 'Here you are!' around midnight, followed by cries as if someone was being strangled. Our local lads saw the dead man and said he resembled the Nastenkos' son, but I'm not sure."

"Nastenko's son!" exclaimed Okhrym and his wife in unison, bursting into bitter tears, for they had hoped to have him as their son-in-law, but now both he and their daughter were in the other world.

"I was heading to the village," the young man continued, "and I met my friend who told me this. So now I'm on my way to Nastenko's to see if his son is at home. I stopped by your place on the way; perhaps you know something about this?"

"No, we don't know anything, dear boy," Okhrym replied. "Please, hurry and tell Nastenko that his son and my daughter are both gone to the next world. Oh, what misery has befallen us!!.."

It was already past midday, and Ivan's father and mother were awaiting his return from the market.

"Why is he taking so long?" Ivan's father said. "He should have been back by now."

Just as he said this, the door creaked open, and a young man entered.

"Good health to you!" he said as he came in. "I've come to inquire about your son."

"Our son went to the market," Ivan's parents replied. "Why do you ask?"

"Well," the young man began, "not far from the main road, they found a dead body that had been torn apart. The man appeared young, and people say he looks exactly like your son."

"Can it really be our son? He left for the market so long ago! It wasn't for nothing that the cuckoo called under our window in the summer – it was foreboding something bad!" Ivan's father exclaimed, and began to weep, his cries echoing through the house. His wife joined him in tears.

"Let's go. Quickly, take us, good lad, to where he lies."

Just as he spoke, someone approached the door and said, "Open up!"

Ivan's mother opened the door, and there... Holy Mother of God! Two constables were holding pieces of Ivan's torn body. They carried him into the house and laid him on the table. The father and mother collapsed breathlessly to the ground when they saw it was their son. People gathered around, started fussing over them, and they began to feel slightly better.

Later, after much crying, Ivan's mother and other women washed and dressed his remains, while his father and other men crafted a coffin for him.

On the third day, the villagers buried Ivan and Oksenia together in a single grave, cursing the witch whom everyone believed was to blame for everything.

Crowds of people attended the funeral. Oh, God almighty, it seemed as if the whole village had gathered. Such a death had drawn everyone's curiosity, and each thought to themselves:

"May merciful God reward them for their sufferings and take them to the Kingdom of Heaven. Since they were separated here by wicked deeds, may they be united there and rejoice, beholding the Righteous God and His Holy Angels!"

Chapter Three
"The Villagers' Revenge"

"Do you see, wife?" Ivan's father asked, looking through the window. "A huge crowd is going somewhere! Is there a burial happening? But no, that can't be right: there are no coffins visible, and the church bells aren't tolling. I'll go out and ask the people what's going on."

"So, old Nastenko went towards the crowd, while his wife, sitting on the bench, mourned her son. She had expected a wedding celebration, but instead, they held a funeral."

Indeed, why had so many people gathered, and where were they heading?

From nearly every household, villagers, both young and old, had come together to see how they would pierce the cursed witch with a stake.

Upon reaching the cemetery, they unearthed a grave and pried open the coffin: inside, the witch's clothes were tattered, and she was lying face down. Everyone there had their suspicions confirmed; undoubtedly, she was the one who had taken Ivan and Oksenia from this world. When they turned her over, they saw blood on her face. All the people were astonished by this.

Two men, cloaked in rags to shield themselves, prepared to stake the witch: they positioned a stake over where her heart would be. As one man held the stake firmly, the other struck it with a hammer; "knock!," and her blood

spurted out. Once the deed was done, they discarded her corpse back into the pit along with the rags they had used for protection. They then filled in the pit and levelled the grave, ensuring no trace of it remained.

The people dispersed, discussing the witch and expressing sympathy for Ivan and Oksenia.

Endnotes

[1] The reference is made to Pentecost, see definition of *Klechalna Sunday* in the Glossary.

[2] The original uses *pereliak*, which is the name of a personified disease caused by a scare; see the definition in the Glossary.

[3] "…a white ball the size of a large head rolled under his feet" – According to Ukrainian folk beliefs, one of the forms witches can take is the form of a ball ("Notes on Ukrainian Demonology" by Vasyl Myloradovych, 2021, Sova Books,

Sydney).

[4] Old Ukrainian traditions frowned upon young people dating on the eve of or during significant religious holidays. According to superstition, such relationships would be doomed to failure. This motif recurs in "The Fire Zmiy" ("Ohnenyi Zmiy," 1841), a novella written by Panteleimon Kulish (1819–1897).

[5] The belief that a witch can only be struck with an aspen stake, and that you can approach her unnoticed only by hiding behind a harrow, is also mentioned in "Notes on Ukrainian Demonology" by Vasyl Myloradovych (2021, Sova Books, Sydney).

[6] It was a widespread belief that when a witch's time comes to die, she experiences agony that can last for days. One way to assist a witch in passing on is to make a hole in the ceiling of the house where she is dying ("Notes on Ukrainian Demonology" by Vasyl Myloradovych, 2021, Sova Books, Sydney).

[7] "Cock-a-doodle-do!" – In Ukrainian, the onomatopoeic word for the noise a rooster makes is "Kukuriku".

The Drowned Maiden

Chapter One
"The Unearthly Encounter with Rusalky"

"How are you, Mykola? Is everything all right?" asked the father, greeting his son who had just returned from the night's lodgings, and, having put the horses in the stable, entered the house.

"Thank God! Our horses are safe, and no beast disturbed them during the night," Mykola replied to his father. "But here's what happened in Chornyi Ravine[8] where we spent the night: almost all the overnighters abandoned their horses and fled the forest."

"What happened there?" Mykola's father asked in surprise.

Lighting his pipe Mykola began to recount his experience.

"Hmm! What? Even now, in the daylight and at

home, it's eerie to speak of it... and last night, we shivered from fright, as if it were the chill of the Epiphany frost. You know," Mykola continued, "the day before yesterday in the forest – what's its name?... Popovyi Forest[9] – where we usually graze the horses. We decided that the next day we would go to Chornyi Ravine because, they say, there's good pasture there. So, yesterday, we went to Chornyi Ravine. After tethering our horses, we picked a spot not far from the deserted house across the pond. Never before had there been such a large gathering as yesterday in Chornyi Ravine: boys from almost the entire village were there.

We made a fire, sat around, and then Yuhym, Tymoshenko's son, said: 'Lads! Why are you sitting idle? You are really fools! Look at this big fire we've made: now it'd be perfect to roast some potatoes. Come on, grab the sacks and head to the village for potatoes – and you don't have to go far: right here at the entrance, there's a huge garden all planted with potatoes.'

"And our lads were just itching for some mischief! Just give them a hint, and they're ready for anything, even to jump into a fire. So, about fifteen lads gathered. Those who had sacks took them, and the rest went without sacks, intending to use their shirts, and briskly headed to the village to steal potatoes. They reached the garden – well, there, of course, some stood watch on every side, while others climbed into the garden. And so the work began!

Our lads got down to business, and without any spades, using just their bare hands, they soon filled either sacks or their shirt fronts, and hurriedly left the garden. Once outside the village, they started singing: they walked joking and laughing – of course, they were young and just wanted to have fun! Some walked ahead, others stayed behind with the sacks. That's when two lads, Antypenko and Perederenko, fell behind the group, staying a bit back. They were carrying potatoes on their shoulders, smoking pipes, and chatting with each other. They were not far from the forest, all the other lads had long since entered the forest, but these two didn't care – just walking leisurely. Then they entered the forest, reached the house near the pond, which had been deserted for a long time.

'Vasyl!' Antypenko's lad said to his friend, 'Look, there's a light in the house! What could that mean? No one has been living here for a long time; unless our lads decided to spend the night there.'

'Indeed, there is a light!' said Vasyl. 'Let's go see what they are doing; but first, let's peek through the window.'

Having said this, both of them went to see what their comrades were doing. They entered the yard, approached the window near the *pokuttia*, and Antypenko's lad was the first to peek through the window... and this was already at midnight.

'Look, Vasyl! It seems like some travelling nobles

have stopped here to spend the night,' he whispered to Perederenko. 'Because there's a candle on the table, and plates, spoons, knives, and forks laid out. And such a huge table with so many plates! Seems like a meal for about twenty people is prepared.'

'Just wait, let me have a look,' Vasyl said to Antypenko, 'what kind of wonder is this?' Then Antypenko's lad stepped back from the window, allowing Perederenko to peer inside. 'What a mystery!' exclaimed Perederenko, 'there's nobody in the house.' With these words, he glanced aside – there by the pich stood a young woman in a white dress, handling pots and ladling food into bowls. She wore

a comb in her hair, and her neck was adorned with so many necklaces that it gleamed like gold!

Perederenko turned away from the window and whispered to his companion, 'Quiet, brother! A young lady appears to be preparing dinner here. Try looking through the other window; let's hope they don't find us: the other nobles must have gone elsewhere.'

Antypenko's lad hurried to the opposite side to peer through the second window – since Perederenko had blocked his view here; he himself wanted a better look at the young woman, especially from the front. Just then, both lads pressed their faces against the window and observed the young woman who, after ladling some food into bowls, placed the ladle back on the pot, took a bowl in each hand, and turned away from the *pich*...

Lord, Thy will be done! The young lady's face and hands were blue as cloth, with water dripping from her mouth.

Our lads then realised who she was: a sort of *rusalka*, and she had even prepared a meal for other *rusalky*. They fled from the spot, leaving their sacks of potatoes behind to escape from such an eerie presence as quickly as possible. After running a significant distance from the house, they looked back, and, oh Lord, Thy will! About twenty maidens in white gowns burst from the forest entrance, and then they watched the *rusalky* enter the house. Antypenko and Perederenko ran to us, as pale as cloth, while we were sitting by the fire roasting potatoes.

'Where did you disappear?' we asked them.

They began to recount what they had seen. Although there were many of us, we were still terribly frightened when we heard that *rusalky* had assembled to dine in that abandoned house. We considered grabbing the horses and quickly fleeing the forest. Yet, we gradually regained our courage, especially since there were older people among us."

'What is there to fear from *rusalky*?' said Vedmid[10] Danylo, an elderly man: 'There are more than one of us here, definitely more than five: Let's lie down and sleep! People say that about five years ago, our Governor's daughter drowned here: she was in this very forest, which still belongs to the Governor, walking with other young women. She wanted to swim and drowned in the ravine not far from the mill, beneath which a willow stands.

No matter how much they searched for her in the water, they never found her. Since then, they say, whoever bathed at that spot drowned every time. Moreover, they say she was such a kind young woman, despite being a drowned maiden, that even now, if someone fearless comes to this forest at midnight, sits under the willow standing above that very ravine where she drowned, and waits for her, exactly at midnight she will emerge from the waters, give you a special garment, dress you up so that you too will appear like a drowned person – see, this is what she does, they say, so that when her friends come out, they won't recognise that you are a living person. Afterwards, she will ask – what do you need from me? You tell her and she will do everything.

'I also know that when my neighbour Zabylenko got into trouble, she warded off all the evil from him. You see, someone hid the body of a murdered man in his barn. He didn't even know, and they blamed all the trouble on him, poor fellow: they accused him of killing the man, and for that, he had to go to Siberia. What to do? He had heard about the Governor's daughter and decided to ask her for help with his misfortune. He went. And what do you think happened? He recounted that she first put on him a dress like hers, and then asked: what does he want from her? He told her everything, and she just said to him, 'Go on, good man, and fear nothing!'

He went home, and the following day they sentenced him to jail; there he would be shackled and sent to Siberia. They were already taking him to jail when on the way they encountered our *otaman*.'

'Wait!' said the *otaman* to the soldiers, who were taking Zabylenko to jail: 'He is innocent; I have learned all about the case. Take him back to court.' The soldiers took him back to court, and there he told the judges how he, while walking through the village yesterday, heard yelling from Seredenko's house. He approached the window and started listening... There, a husband and wife were arguing, and the woman, in anger, told her husband: 'You dog, stop beating me, or tomorrow I'll reveal how you killed a Russian to take his money, and even put his body in someone else's barn. Now an innocent man will perish because of you.'

Well, the judges ordered the court officer to bring Seredenko to court, and they released Zabylenko. The following day, the court officer, along with the constables, brought Seredenko, who confessed to everything when interrogated in court. He was sent to Siberia, while Zabylenko was released as an innocent man.

'See, boys!', said Vedmid Danylo: 'how good this maiden is: she orchestrated everything so that the man started beating his wife, who then revealed everything, and just then, the *otaman* happened to overhear it all. So why should we be afraid?'

Our lads, hearing this, felt somewhat encouraged, and together, including me, we went to see if it was true that there was light in that house. Indeed, there was light.

✳✳✳

"So, you see," Mykola told his father, "that's what happened to us yesterday. Our lads say that from now on, none of them will set foot in the Chornyi Ravine."

Mykola's father was amazed by what his son had told him, and then he himself began to speak about what he had heard about the Governor's daughter.

Chapter Two
"Love Confession in the Forest"

"Marusia, hey!... Vivdia, hey!..." the girls called out, walking through the forest. Excited by the arrival of spring and the forest turning green, they had immediately ventured to pick flowers – because always, as soon as spring begins, they gather and go to the forest. Now, the girls were dispersed throughout the forest, searching for flowers.

"Priska, hey!... Vivdia, hey!... Marta, hey!..." Marusia called out as she walked and picked flowers, but no response came.

"I must have strayed too far from the others," Marusia thought to herself, still looking for flowers; and again she called: "Priska, hey!... Oksana, hey!... Hana, hey!..." Still, no one replied to Marusia's calls. Then, suddenly, a voice called out: "Hey!..." She looked around and saw a young man not far from her, dressed in a white shirt and red belt, who seemed to be picking flowers.

"Good day to you, by God's grace!" the young man greeted Marusia as he approached, to which she responded, "Thank you!" Catching a glimpse of him, she blushed – her heart ached deeply for this young man, whom she had seen several times at church, and he had truly captured her affection.

"What are you doing walking alone here?" the young man inquired.

"I'm not alone!" said Marusia, "There are many of us girls around, but it seems I've wandered far from them."

Marusia continued to pick flowers, stealing glances

at the young man. "He's so handsome!" she thought, for indeed the young man was striking: bright eyes, rosy cheeks, and tall stature.

"What's your name, girl?" the young man asked.

"Marusia. And why do you wish to know my name?" she asked, her cheeks colouring.

Noticing this, he stepped closer and said, "Just so! I ask because you, you see, are so beautiful, and if you were my wife, I would be the happiest man alive, and you would be the most cherished in the world to me."

That was precisely what Marusia hoped to hear, and without any hesitation, she quickly responded: "Could it be that you are deceiving me and aiming to mock a girl?"

And seeing this, he asked her, "Would you truly agree to marry me?"

"What a wonder," Marusia responded, delighted that such a handsome young man was proposing to her – for she had often seen him at church and thought to herself, "What if he were my husband!" And that's why she was so talkative, even though it was uncommon for a girl to converse so openly with a young man, especially considering she had seen him at church but didn't know who he was.

"If you don't mind," said the young man to Marusia, "take these flowers that I picked for you – because I saw you going into the forest and I followed you."

"Thank you!" said Marusia, accepting the flowers, and then she asked, "What is your name?"

"My name is Hrytsko, but they call me Perepechenko," the young man replied.

"Then you, Hrytsko, are hurting me," Marusia said, "implying that I would dislike your flowers. Oh, Hrytsko, if only you knew how long my heart has been aching for you! That first time last year when I saw you in church, you seemed the best of all to me, and since then I've thought only of you, not even knowing who you were."

"I too have longed for you, Marusia, and many times, I wanted to confess my love, but I never saw you around, as I had only recently returned from the Don. Although I knew your father, I feared he would refuse when I asked for his daughter's hand – I was orphaned after my parents passed and had little to my name: just a small piece of land and a few cattle. So I decided to first go to the Don to earn some money. God helped me – I made about five hundred rubles and now have returned home to buy more livestock and then to ask for your hand, first from you and then from your father. And now, what do I see? You love me, Marusia. Oh, how fortunate I am! Tell me, Marusia, do you love me?"

Marusia blushed and said, "I love you and will love you forever! I will marry no one but you."

Hrytsko embraced Marusia and kissed her. "And I swear to you, Marusia, to be faithful and cherish you until the cold earth separates us! Now, my dear, I will strive to acquire a decent herd of livestock, and then, if God grants us health, I will send my *starosty* to you." At that moment, Hrytsko took a ring off his finger and gave it to Marusia, and she gave him hers.

"Hey, Marusia!" a girl's voice called out not far from our lovers. Thinking that if someone saw him with Marusia, it might start gossip that would be bad for her, Hrytsko kissed her and said, "Farewell, Marusia! Come out to this forest again tomorrow, we'll meet here."

Marusia replied, "Very well, Hrytsko." After one more kiss, they parted, both happy: Hrytsko went in one direction, and Marusia went towards where her friend had called. Soon, Vivdia emerged from behind the bushes.

"Where have you been?" Marusia asked her. "I called out so many times, but no one answered, you must have gone far. Let's go home – it's getting late." Then they started calling out, and soon all the girls gathered , and singing songs, they made their way home.

Soon the whole village was abuzz with the news that Hrytsko Perepechenko, once an orphan and poor – with nothing left after his parents passed – had now accumulated a substantial amount of livestock. He had bought fields, various cattle – horses, a pair of oxen, and perhaps ten sheep. There was no denying it: he had become a wealthy farmer. Everyone envied and praised him for being such a fine farmer, especially being so young. Everyone began to respect him, and Marusia's father often spoke of Hrytsko, marvelling at how he had managed to prosper despite his initial poverty, and he would have been happy if God sent him such a son-in-law.

Marusia was pleased that people spoke so highly of Hrytsko, including her father, who praised him as a good farmer. Everything was going well, and soon Hrytsko was supposed to get married – but then a great misfortune befell him. A conscription for soldiers began, and Hrytsko, as the representative of his family, had to enlist. Though he had uncles with sons, none were suitable, so it inevitably fell to Hrytsko to join the army.

So, it happened! The drafting of soldiers had begun, and no matter how much Hrytsko tried to evade capture, he was eventually found and shackled.

That evening, Marusia sat by the window in her house, sewing a *sorochka*; her mother was also busy with some household tasks, while her father was away. Marusia's thoughts were consumed by Hrytsko: it had been ages since she had seen him – he had told her he would be hiding to avoid conscription. She constantly feared his capture. As this worry overwhelmed her, tears began to stream down her face.

"Why are you crying, daughter?" her mother inquired, noticing that Marusia was wiping away her tears. Marusia then opened up about her fears: she loved Hrytsko deeply, and now he might be taken away to serve as a soldier, which would leave her life filled with tears and regret.

Her mother felt a pang of sympathy as her daughter began to cry, because she had hoped for Hrytsko to become her son-in-law.

"Don't cry, my daughter," Marusia's mother said: "I know he is a fine man and it would fill me with joy to see my daughter married to such a person in my old age. Perhaps God will intervene, and he will avoid the draft.

Such a fine farmer he has become! Just as he got everything established, this calamity strikes."

"Mum, do you hear that?" Marusia said to her mother, "It sounds like shackles clanging on the street: they must be leading more conscripts past our house." She peered out the window and, to her dismay, saw a group of about twenty conscripts being led by, with Hrytsko at the forefront, shackled to another young man. Marusia shuddered at the sight of her beloved Hrytsko. "Oh heavens!" she exclaimed and suddenly fainted. Her mother, greatly alarmed by the sudden collapse, didn't immediately grasp the cause. She lifted Marusia, laid her on a bench, and gave her some water. Marusia's heart thudded wildly as she lay nearly unconscious.

The door creaked open... Marusia's mother looked up to see Hrytsko standing there in iron shackles, the reason for her daughter's distress now painfully clear.

"Greetings and farewell!" Hrytsko announced as he entered, "you won't see me again – I've been conscripted. Where is Marusia?" he inquired with a heavy sigh.

Marusia's mother recounted everything – how Marusia had been sitting by the window, and upon glimpsing him in chains, screamed and tumbled to the floor. Hrytsko walked over to where Marusia lay: "Farewell, my sweetheart," he murmured as he looked down at her, tears streaming down his face, "We may never see each other again!"

Witnessing the scene, Marusia's mother also began to weep.

Marusia remained unconscious until a faint stir awakened her; slowly, she opened her eyes... "My God! What do I see?" she exclaimed upon seeing Hrytsko in chains. "Oh! Without you, Hrytsko, I cannot live! I would rather die than be separated from you!" She wept as though she were a child, and tears welled up in Hrytsko's eyes too. The guards, who had entered with Hrytsko to keep watch, and Hrytsko's fellow conscript, moved by the scene, found themselves tearing up as well.

The guards told Hrytsko it was time to leave. After bidding farewell to Marusia's mother, Hrytsko approached Marusia and said, "Farewell, Marusia!" They embraced and kissed, both of them crying. "I will love you forever, Marusia, and only death in war can separate us!

"I cannot live without you, Hrytsko!" Marusia exclaimed. "To me, death is preferable to parting from you." She then burst into tears.

"Goodbye, Marusia!" Hrytsko sobbed. "The day after tomorrow, they might shave my head." Marusia had gotten up but then she fainted again, collapsing onto the bench, and did not hear Hrytsko as he left the house.

Chapter Three
"In Search for Patronage"

The sun had long since set; everyone in the village was asleep, except for the occasional fire still flickering here and there; the overnighters with their horses had arrived hours ago. Who is it then, walking along the road that leads to Chornyi Ravine, heading straight into the forest despite the common fear of even stepping near it – fuelled by rumours spread throughout the village about what the overnighters witnessed in the abandoned house, making everyone too scared to approach by day, much less at night? Who is this brave soul, and why do they venture into the forest at such a late hour? It is the wretched Marusia, seeking out the drowned maiden to plead for her Hrytsko release from conscription, to spare him this calamity – inspired by the stories she heard about the drowned maiden, who is said to bring good to all, even saving Zabylenko from Siberia. And where is her Hrytsko? Tomorrow, they will take him in for processing and shave his head.

"…And then I will be left alone," Marusia thought. "No! Even though it's terrifying, I will go to the drowned maiden, fall at her feet, and plead for her to free my Hrytsko! She is so kind, she won't harm me. I must go – I will run as fast as I can – whatever happens, I must see the kind drowned maiden."

With this resolve, Marusia quickened her pace: the forest loomed ahead, and she entered it. It was daunting for her to walk at such an hour. And to whom was she walking? To a maiden from the other world! Yet, what other option

did she have? She felt a profound pity for Hrytsko: she was willing to go through fire for him. Crossing herself, Marusia pressed forward.

She arrived at the house where she had heard there was recently a light and where rusalky were seen in the evenings. A shiver ran through Marusia's body. 'Maybe I will die here!' Marusia considered. 'Well, so be it! I would rather die at the hands of rusalky than live in the world without my beloved Hrytsko!'

Now she had reached the dam, and before her stood the willow over the cliff where the Governor's daughter had drowned. Marusia approached the willow and boldly took her place under it, awaiting the drowned maiden. It was undoubtedly late: the water remained still. She felt sorrowful, her heart thudded intensely, but there was nothing else she could do! She felt torn between fleeing from these eerie places and staying to wait for the drowned maiden. Her gaze fixed only on the water, the home of the kind drowned maiden.

Suddenly, out of nowhere, a boat appeared, with a maiden in a white dress sitting in it, for in the moonlight everything could be clearly seen. She rowed, guiding the boat straight towards the willow under which poor Marusia sat. Marusia was scared at first, but then thought: "What do I have to fear? One cannot die seven times – there is only one death!"

The boat reached the shore, and the maiden, seated in it, disembarked, and approached Marusia – who had already stood up and was waiting for her, ready to prostrate herself at her feet – and said, "What do you need from me, girl? Speak – I will do all I can." Upon hearing this, Marusia grew slightly braver and, crying bitterly, threw herself at the feet of the drowned maiden. "Don't bow to me!" the drowned maiden told Marusia, "We don't tolerate bowing here – they are only suitable for your world. Stand up and speak: what do you need?"

"Dear maiden, my dove!" Marusia said, rising to her feet, "Don't leave me alone in my sorrow! I loved and still love Hrytsko, but they are taking him away from me: they have seized him, put him in chains, and tomorrow they will take him to the army. I may never see him again! Please,

don't forsake me, maiden! Save Hrytsko from conscription; I can't live a day without him!" Marusia wept bitterly.

"Don't cry!" said the drowned maiden. "I see how your heart is aching for him, and I will ensure that Hrytsko remains alive."

Upon hearing this, Marusia was so overwhelmed with joy that she didn't know what to do and fell at her feet again – thump!

"Don't bow!" the drowned maiden said. "In your world, bows can achieve anything, but not in ours! Now listen, I'm going to tell you what to do next: My friends will soon arrive. Don't be afraid of them. To ensure they don't recognise you, just wait – I will bring you our dress. Remove your own and leave it here under the willow. We will dine in that house, and you will join us. After we've dined, they will leave, and I'll tell you what to do next. Don't be afraid! Your Hrytsko will be with you!" Having said that, she dived into the water!... and fetched a white dress, just like hers. "Take off your clothes!" she told Marusia. Marusia removed all her clothes, and the drowned maiden handed her the dress she had retrieved from the water. Marusia put it on, so overjoyed that Hrytsko would be with her, she did not even care that a revenant was helping her into the dress.

"Don't fear anything!" the drowned maiden reassured Marusia. "My companions won't recognize you – they'll think you recently drowned. If they ask, just tell them you went swimming and drowned. They will truly believe it and won't bother you. Look, here sail my friends!"

Marusia looked – suddenly, as far as the eye could see, the water was covered with boats, and the girls were arriving in dresses exactly like those worn by the Governor's daughter and her.

They arrived, disembarked, took each other by the hands and went in pairs to the house, and the Governor's daughter took Marusia by the hand and went with her.

When Marusia first passed by the house, it had been dark, but now she saw it was lit inside. They reached the house and entered. Marusia observed that the table was set with a candle and a plate, spoon, fork, and knife for each guest, just as it would be at a nobleman's house. Everyone sat down at the table, including Marusia.

"See, I guessed right," said the Governor's daughter. "I decided to add an extra plate; today we've been joined by another soul." The Governor's daughter, whom Marusia had known when she was alive and often seen in church, pointed Marusia out to her companions. They began to ask her how she had drowned. Feeling fearless with the Governor's daughter by her side, Marusia told them she had gone for a swim but then drowned.

They began to dine, and what a splendid feast it

was! The table was laden with various dishes, all featuring fresh fish, and there were crayfish too, but no bread was served. After they finished eating, the Governor's daughter announced, "Let's go – it's time for us to return home!"

As soon as she said this, everything disappeared in an instant: the candle, the plates... all vanished, leaving only the visible cracks in the walls of the long-abandoned house.

They exited the house, and the drowned women went their way, while the Governor's daughter stayed behind with Marusia, walking quietly together. When they reached the willow, all the boats were gone, except for the one the Governor's daughter had arrived in. She told Marusia, "Now take off my dress and put on yours." Marusia did as told, handed back the dress to the drowned maiden, and dressed in her own clothes.

"Wait here for me!" the drowned maiden told Marusia. "I'll be right back," and she plunged into the water like a diver. Marusia stood under the willow, waiting for her return, when shortly afterward, the drowned maiden re-emerged from the water carrying some sort of note.

"Here, take this note," the drowned maiden told Marusia, "Bring it to my father and give it to him; and now – farewell!"

"Farewell, kind lady!" said Marusia, securing the note in her bosom: "May God bless you for your kindness!"

"Do not fear! Your Hrytsko will not be drafted into the army," assured the drowned maiden, before she boarded the boat and rowed away, while Marusia, filled with joy, hurriedly left the forest.

Chapter Four
"Together at Last"

Lunch was over. The Governor, having dined and rested, got up and went to his scribe, who was located in a small cottage on his estate, busily working with his quill pen. He too began to engage in work: he started dictating – what an intelligent man he was! He came up with ideas on his own, not even reading from any document or the like, but inventing from his own mind, and his scribe recorded on paper what he was saying. Just then, the Governor's footman came in and said, "Sir, my apologies, but a young lady is asking for you and says she urgently needs to see you."

"What young lady?" the Governor inquired of his footman. "Let her come in here." The footman exited, and soon the young woman entered the Governor's chambers. This young lady was our Marusia – she had brought the

Governor the note given to her by the drowned maiden.

"What do you need?" the Governor asked Marusia as she entered the room.

Marusia first bowed deeply to the Governor, then said:

"I am at your mercy." She pulled a handkerchief from her bosom, unfolded it, and handed him the note wrapped within. The Governor took the note, shook his head, and began to open it. As he did, something else wrapped in a small piece of paper fell out. He picked it up, set it aside without opening it, and began reading the note. "What is this? I recognise this handwriting, yet I can't place it," the Governor remarked, and he read on. The note contained a plea for him to endeavour to release Hrytsko Perepechenko from conscription.

After reading the note and pondering who might have written it, as there was no signature or name, the Governor then unwrapped the small piece of paper... and God's will! The Governor turned as pale as a sheet. From the paper, he extracted a ring that he recognised as his daughter's, which she always wore and with which she had drowned. He now understood that his daughter had written the note; he trembled, overwhelmed by the shock, and said nothing more to Marusia except: "Go on your way! I will do everything as written here; I will free Hrytsko Perepechenko from conscription: I will find someone to take his place!"

Marusia was overjoyed to hear the Governor promise to free Hrytsko, and she left the chamber cheerfully and went home."

And where was Hrytsko? He had long been in the city, dreading the next day – conscription day – as if it were his death. So many conscripts had been gathered from all the districts. The air was filled with cries and loud voices as mothers, sisters, brothers, and wives came to bid farewell – for among those taken were many married men. Amidst this commotion, nobody cried for Hrytsko; he was an orphan. Though he had uncles, what did it matter? They were actually relieved that he was taken for conscription, thankful that their own sons were not taken – since all their sons were unfit: some too young, disabled, or otherwise unfit for service. So, Hrytsko, a fine young man, was destined for the army. He wept bitterly, mourning the life he was leaving behind, especially parting from his beloved Marusia. But what could he do? Such was his fate.

The next day, they were brought in for induction. Each recruit was examined by the doctors who would either declare "forehead" for some and "back of the head!" for others. Those who heard "back of the head" were overjoyed, leaving the place without looking back, thanking God for sparing them from military service. Hrytsko heard that they had begun to process the conscripts from his district. His heart pounded fiercely... and then – "Hrytsko Perepechenko!" the clerk called out, and Hrytsko's heart skipped a beat. Then, what a miracle! Just as his name was read, the Governor stood up from his seat and announced, "Wait! I have hired a substitute for him. Release him!"

At that moment, the Governor ordered that Hrytsko's substitute be brought in. They shaved his head and had him ready, while Hrytsko was released. Hrytsko felt as if he was floating; the ground seemed to vanish beneath his feet! He longed to fall at the Governor's feet and thank him for his immense mercy, but that proved impossible! The area was crowded with nobles, and he felt overwhelmed: their gold trappings sparkled so brightly. Hrytsko couldn't understand why the Governor had shown him such mercy.

Hrytsko didn't linger there; he hurried home as fast as he could. He reached his village and immediately headed to the house of Marusia's father: his heart yearning to see his beloved Marusia. He was unsure whether she was well, as she had been unconscious when he left her. Marusia was sitting on a bench, lost in thoughts of Hrytsko, when suddenly the door creaked and there he stood before her. Marusia was overjoyed and instantly rushed to embrace and kiss him.

Later, Hrytsko shared the entire ordeal, still astonished and puzzled as to why the Governor had shown him such kindness. Marusia revealed everything to him: how she had visited the drowned maiden, the Governor's daughter, and how the maiden had written a note to her father, which led the Governor to hire a substitute for Hrytsko.

"And you, my sweetheart, weren't afraid to go to the drowned maiden?" Hrytsko asked Marusia.

"I wasn't scared of anything," Marusia replied. "I would do anything to free you from conscription."

Hrytsko wept because he felt deeply moved that Marusia had risked her life for him; he held Marusia tight and kissed her.

A week later, Hrytsko and Marusia were wed. They celebrated their union and prayed to the Merciful Lord to bless the kind, drowned maiden for bringing them everlasting happiness.

Endnotes

[8] Chornyi Ravine – "Chornyi" translates from Ukrainian as "black".

[9] Popovyi Forest – "Popovyi" in Ukrainian means "belonging to a priest", i.e., "priest's".

[10] Vedmid – "Vedmid" translates from Ukrainian as "bear".

Easy Come, Easy Go

In a certain village lived a man whose name I couldn't tell you... Let's call him Ivan, as every village surely has many Ivans. He had a wife and probably no fewer than four children. So, he had a family, but what of it? He was indifferent to them, consumed by his drinking, a drunkard of such degree that the world seldom saw his like. He squandered all his livestock on *horilka*, wore shabby clothes; his wife and small children wandered barefoot and threadbare. Daily, he'd return home drunk, and start beating his wife, demanding, "Why haven't you cooked dinner or supper?"

He was oblivious to the fact that there was nothing at home, not even a pinch of salt, and his wife and children remained hungry, often going two days without even

a glimpse of bread. His wife would only weep, and that was all; all he cared about was how to get drunk, and he would secretly take whatever was left of her possessions – *plakhta*, *sorochka*, *ochipok*, or kerchief – and pawn them at the tavern.

One day, when his wife opened the trunk, she discovered it empty, finding nothing inside. She wept and cursed her fate for marrying such a lazy man. "What should I do?" she wondered, for by now her husband had squandered both his inheritance and hers. The only property she had left was the garden, where she grew hemp, cabbage, beets, and potatoes. This provided her with something to cook, but even that had been mortgaged last year.

No matter how much money he received, he spent it all on *horilka*, leaving her destitute. With no other choice, his wife went with their children, resorted to begging for bread from house to house for the sake of Christ, as they were on the verge of starving to death. Her husband, however, remained uncaring about that: he would steal something and immediately head to the tavern, drink himself senseless, and not have a worry in the world. Sometimes he wouldn't see a crumb of bread for days, but as long as he had his *horilka*, that was all that mattered to him. Occasionally, our Ivan would get so drunk that he would be thrown out of the tavern or would start a fight or argument at someone's house and be kicked out all the same; he would stagger down the street, and collapse somewhere near a fence, falling asleep. He had been warned repeatedly to stop drinking, but he heeded no one: even the village head had urged him to quit, warning that he would be conscripted into the army the moment the draft was called.

So, what then? Our Ivan, despite his heavy drinking, was cunning. Whenever conscription started, he would stop drinking, and sometimes even go two weeks without a drink. But as soon as the conscription ended, he would return to his old ways. He couldn't fool the village head forever, and on the second or third year, they would have conscripted him, however his addiction to the damned *horilka* had so strong that he no longer resembled a proper

man; besides, his frequent brawls had left him with broken arms and legs, making him utterly useless and certainly unfit for military service.

He was even whipped in the village for his drinking, but it didn't matter. Even if they had killed him, he would still do the same thing: keep drinking *horilka*. His clothes were tattered, but he never stopped drinking. The villagers harboured no sympathy for him, but they did pity his wife and children.

Ivan's wife, who came from a good family and whose father was a prosperous man, was now reduced to begging near the hospital with her children. A neighbour, a wealthy man, took Ivan's wife and children off the streets, brought them into his home, and provided them with food and drink. He promised that if they behaved well and did not follow in their father's footsteps, he would bequeath all his livestock to them. Although he was married, he had no children of his own and was getting on in years. Ivan's wife and children were delighted and left the hospital to live with this man. They respected and obeyed him in all matters as though he were their own father.

"I'm going," said a dead-drunk Ivan to the tavern keeper as he staggered out of the tavern, "to watch boys and girls jump over the fire."

You see, he had glimpsed through the window a bonfire blazing in the village by the pond. It was *Ivan*

Kupalo Night, and all the boys and girls had been up all night: weaving wreaths, piling up a huge stack of wood, lighting it, and jumping over the fire – as is the custom in Ukraine.

Our Ivan, wanting to watch the festivities of the boys and girls, put on his hat and left the tavern. He might have stayed longer and probably spent the night there, but the tavern keeper, having seen him there all day and even napping in her establishment, needed to rest from her daily burdens (after all, she had been on her feet all day long: constantly dispensing *horilka*) – so she finally ushered him out. Ivan then left the building, singing loudly, "Oh, *chumak, chumak*! Why haven't you returned early from Crimea?" and staggered toward where the bonfire burned and the boys and girls were merrymaking.

"Hello!" Ivan exclaimed as he approached the fire, where boys and girls were leaping like frogs: "So, I've come to check out what you're doing here?"

"Hello, Ivan!" the boys and girls yelled back, bursting into laughter at his wobbly stance – he was so saturated with vodka!

"Now would be the time," laughed one of the young men, "for him, in his drunken state, to go into the forest for the fern flower. They say that if you go to the forest at midnight and pluck this plant, whatever you wish for will come true. You'll have so much money that not even the entire state could match it. Let him go! Nothing scares him now – he's so drunk that he can barely stand on his feet." After saying this, the young man and others approached the drunk Ivan and said to him:

"Hey, Ivan, would you want to be happy – to have so much money you couldn't possibly spend it all?"

"Why wouldn't I want money?" Ivan responded. "But how would I get it – I'd be ready for anything!"

"Well, if you want it," the young men said again, "we'll teach you. Listen! Do you know the fern that grows in the forest, and also in gardens?"

"How could I not know it!" Ivan exclaimed, thrilled, as he strongly desired money: he would then never run out of *horilka* at home. "I could afford *varenukha* too!" he thought.

"My wife once pointed it out to me," Ivan said, "and told me that no person can pull it out on *Ivan Kupalo Night*[11] at midnight."

"Did she tell you anything else about this flower?" the young men asked Ivan.

"No, nothing!" Ivan replied.

"So, here's what…" the young men told him, "It can be pull out, but you need to know how to do it. As soon as you pull it out, you must run from the forest without looking back. No matter who calls you or what appears before you, keep running and don't look back, because if you do, everything will be lost, and you will be doomed! And if you don't look back and manage to bring the fern flower out of the forest, then you'll get as much money as you desire. So, Ivan, if you want, go to any forest, even this one beyond the village, and pull out the fern flower, but be sure not to look back, no matter what appears."

Ivan listened to the young men, not knowing how to contain his excitement thinking, "What is there to fear? Perhaps unclean spirits? I'll just cross myself and they'll vanish. If not, I'll take a sturdy club with me and strike anything that comes my way, even the *chort* himself. I won't back down! There's no joking with me when I'm on a mission, especially if anyone tries to snatch the fern flower from me so I won't have any money! Bloody *chort* already has plenty of money, but won't share with us, people, even a little! No, I'm not afraid of you!" Ivan exclaimed and told the young men, "Thank you, lads, for telling me how to get the money. So, what do you think, is it almost midnight?" Ivan asked them.

"It probably is already," the young men replied.

"Well, that's great, if it's indeed midnight!" Ivan exclaimed. "Farewell! I'm off..." and with that, he hurried toward the forest beyond the village.

"He's so drunk he's really going to look for the fern flower!" the young men remarked after Ivan had left. "Let's hope he doesn't get killed. Otherwise, we'll be blamed for sending him into the forest."

Soon, Ivan reached the forest. He entered and wandered through, searching for the fern flower. Whenever he tore out a plant, he would hold it up to his eyes and check in the moonlight to see what kind of herb he had picked.

"This is it!" Ivan exclaimed, finally pulling out a fern flower and inspecting it. "Now I have no worries. I'd better head straight home!" No sooner had Ivan spoken these words than dogs started barking and howling from one side, cats meowed from another, and a whistling noise echoed through the forest like human voices... Ivan, heeding the young men's advice, didn't look back and continued to hasten out of the forest. He could hear something screeching like an owl nearby and felt like someone was chasing him, with dogs following close behind... but he kept moving forward without looking back.

"No, I won't turn around!" Ivan thought to himself. "Do whatever you want! The devil's brood, you want me to drop the fern flower, but no, that won't happen: you've picked the wrong one to mess with!" Just then, he heard his wife's voice calling him from behind, "Ivan, wait! Why are you leaving me alone?" Ivan nearly stopped upon hearing his wife's voice, thinking perhaps she had been out and was coming home late. But then he remembered that the *chort* could shape-shift into anyone and kept walking without looking back. He thought he heard his eldest son crying out behind him, "Dad, wait for me! The wolves will eat me if left alone." He also heard someone rushing after him, yelling, "Stop! You won't escape!... I got you! Hey, you, hey, hey, hey!.."

Ivan felt as if dogs were snapping at his heels. "No, you won't fool me!" he thought. "I won't let go of the fern flower!" He tightened his grip on the fern flower. "And if you dare come closer, even if you're *chorty* and fiends, I'll strike you with this club so hard that your eyes will pop out!" he said aloud, swinging the club in his hand. Just as he emerged from the forest, everything behind him

fell silent, as if nothing had ever happened. "Thank God!" Ivan exclaimed. "Now I'll live like a lord!"

But no sooner had he said this than Ivan noticed someone approaching him, appearing like any other person. As the figure came closer, Ivan saw not a peasant, but a gentleman dressed in a black coat, like our magistrate's, with a black hat on his head.

"Good health to you, man!" the nobleman said to Ivan as they approached each other. "What do you wish from me? Speak, and whatever you desire will instantly appear before you."

Ivan realised that the fern flower had given him this power to make this nobleman stand before him and inquire about his needs.

He replied, "What do I wish? Give me money; I need nothing else!" The nobleman took out a small purse from his pocket and handed it to Ivan.

"Here's your money," the nobleman told him. "With this, you can buy anything you wish; you may fill up whole barrels with money, and this pouch will never go empty. Live and enjoy life!.. but in return, you owe me a favour in ten years."

"What favour do I owe you?" Ivan asked, delighted to have the money in hand. "I'll thank you in any way you want, what do you need?"

"You will repay me with nothing more than your soul," said the nobleman.

Hearing this, Ivan grew a little frightened. He now realised that it was an unclean spirit endowing him with money – as only Satan takes one's soul in exchange for money. Ivan pondered over the grim prospect of giving his soul to the *chort* and spending eternity in hell. After some thought, he said to himself, "Fine! I'll outsmart you, even if you're the *chort*! I'll tell him to come for my soul in fifteen years, not ten He reasoned that in fifteen years, the *chort* would forget about it. "How could he remember everyone he's given money to? After all, even I can barely remember what happened last year. I'm sure in fifteen years he'll forget! I know he will!" And then he said:

"Fine! I'll give you my soul, but I have one request: instead of taking my soul in ten years, take it in fifteen." Ivan said to the *chort*.

The *chort* thought about it for a moment before replying,

"Very well! For you, I'm willing to agree to this. We'll have an excellent time then! For now, I'll visit you regularly, so make sure you prepare something to entertain me with. Afterward, I'll invite you to my place. Now, go home, get ready, buy everything you need, and expect me to come the day after tomorrow. I will surely come to see you."

"Agreed!" said Ivan.

"Farewell then!" said the *chort*. "We'll see each other soon..." and he walked towards the forest where Ivan had gone searching for the fern flower, while Ivan headed back to the village.

As soon as he arrived, he went straight to the tavern. He sat on the bench and ordered half a quart of *horilka* for seven kopiyky. The tavern keeper, knowing that if she didn't collect money from him upfront, would never see it, told him, "Give me the money first, and then I'll pour you some *horilka*."

"Money?" said Ivan, "Here, take these coins!" He pulled a small pouch from his pocket and spilled not only coins but also chervontsi onto the table. "See how much money I have, and you were hesitant to give me even a half a quart!"

The tavern keeper was stunned to see Ivan, the impoverished drunkard now pouring out chervontsi on the table, perhaps a whole hundred. She quickly measured out the half a quart for him.

"Here, Ivan, have some lovely *horilka*! I have infused it with herbs just for you," the tavern keeper said, placing a bottle with the beverage.

You see, the damned tavern keeper was trying to curry favour with our Ivan. Seeing his money she quickly poured him a generous amount of quality infused *horilka*, when previously she would have given him the worst homebrew, diluted with water. "Don't you want something to eat?" the tavern keeper asked Ivan. "I have some leftover *pampushky* from yesterday, I saved them especially for you because I knew you'd come today."

She served him a plate of *pampushky*, and Ivan enjoyed them while drinking his *horilka*. After finishing the drink, Ivan said to the tavern keeper...

"Here, take a chervonets for yourself, and use the rest to measure out as much *horilka* as possible. I need enough for tomorrow because I'm expecting guests. A nobleman who generously gifted me money will be coming, and I want to thank him."

The tavern keeper asked, "What kind nobleman gave you so much money?"

Ivan replied, "What good nobleman? He wasn't good at first but was forced to become good!" And Ivan then recounted everything to the tavern keeper: how he had gone to the forest at midnight seeking the fern flower, the strange experiences he had there, how he had encountered a nobleman upon leaving the forest, who gave him this money, in exchange for his soul, which he had agreed to surrender in fifteen years.

"Well, even you'll agree, Khyvra, that in fifteen years he won't remember he gave me money!" Ivan chuckled to the tavern keeper. "Here's how fools are fooled! Ha! Ha! Ha!.. and he wantcd, you know, for me to give him my soul

94

in ten years, but no way; he's smart, but maybe I'm smarter than him!"

The tavern keeper was astonished at what Ivan was saying, and at first, she hesitated to accept the chervontsi because she knew they were given to him by the *chort*. However, she eventually decided to take the money, reasoning that money was still money all.

He entered the house and said, "Good health to you, my wife, and you children! Let's go straight home; we'll live in comfort now – we have all we need for food and drink." And he pulled out from his pocket a purse full of coins and showed them to his wife and children. They were overjoyed to see how much money their father had, and they started asking him where he got it all, and he told them everything.

He entered the house and said, "Good health to you, my wife, and you children! Let's go straight home; we'll live in comfort now – we have all we need for food and drink." And he pulled out from his pocket a purse full of coins and showed them to his wife and children. They were overjoyed to see how much money their father had, and they started asking him where he got it all, and he told them everything.

The wife and children were a bit afraid that it might be *chort's* money, and that he sold his soul to the *chort* for it, however they were all willing, especially when he assured them that the *chort* might forget he ever gave him the money.

After thanking their neighbour for his hospitality, Ivan and his family went back home. When they arrived, they found the windows smashed, and all the benches stolen. Ivan repaired the windows and made new benches, and then he started thinking about how to manage the household.

"But first," he thought, "I need to prepare for tomorrow – the one who gave me this money will visit me."

He quickly bought everything needed: meat, *horilka*, and all sorts of things for the occasion. He also decided to get new clothes for himself, his wife, and their children since their old ones were worn. Ivan went to the market and instructed his wife to have everything ready for the evening, as the guests were expected to arrive around midnight.

Ivan went to the town, while his wife stayed at home, cooking and baking all sorts of things. She sat on the bench, waiting for her husband to return from the market. So, towards evening, Ivan returned. He bought his wife a *plakhta*, *zapaska*, and *yupka*. He bought a *svyta* for each of his children and, for himself, he bought not a *svyta* but a blue *zhupan*. No longer hesitant about spending money, he wanted to show off his fine *zhupan*. They all dressed up, lit a candle, set the table, and waited for their guests.

They waited for a long time, but the guests never arrive. The village had gone to sleep, with no lights in sight, yet still no sign of the guests.

Ivan's wife and children fell asleep wherever they could. Only Ivan remained awake, he could not sleep: sitting at the table, with a bottle of *horilka*, *kovbasa*, and *salo* laid out in front of him.

Suddenly, he heard someone knocking on his gate. He stood up and went to open it.

"Good health to you, Ivan," said the same man, who had given him the money as he entered the house.

"Good health to you, kind sir!" Ivan replied. He knew that it was the *chort* who had come to him, yet he still addressed him politely "sir" because the man was dressed in a fine *zhupan*, resembling a well-to-do nobleman. "Why have you been so delayed? My wife and children have already fallen asleep waiting for you. Just wait, I'll wake them up."

"No! There's no need to wake them." the *chort* replied, "Let them sleep; we can have a good time without them!"

"Please, sit down," Ivan said to the *chort*: "and let's have a drink."

"Eh!" said the *chort*: "so you've prepared everything already; well, thank you for that! When you come to my place, I'll treat you."

"And where do you live?" Ivan asked, pouring a glass.

"I have many houses – I live all over the earth: today here, and tomorrow elsewhere. But let's not dwell on that! Come to the same forest where you were the day before yesterday. I have an estate there too."

"Where exactly?" Ivan asked him: "I've been in that forest many times, but I've never noticed any house there; was it built recently?"

"Yes, not so long ago," replied the *chort*.

"Well, that may be," Ivan said. "But for now, let's have a drink!" He poured a glass, raised it to his mouth, and said, "To your health!" and drank it, and then offered a drink to the *chort*.

"To your health!" said the *chort*, drinking the *horilka*. "Let's have another one."

Ivan poured another glass, then another, and another... Ivan was getting drunk. They ate well, and then they drank more, leaving Ivan extremely drunk."

"Ah, if only we had music now!" said Ivan, getting up from the table and placing his hands on his hips: "I would now dance a *tropak*, like there's no tomorrow!"

"Do you want music to play?" the *chort* asked. "So, what's the matter? Hey, you!.."

Just as the *chort* uttered those words – from behind the *pich* and under the floorboards there erupted a clatter, a rumble, a booming sound... Who knows where it all came from! Musicians emerged from behind the *pich* with violins, *bandury*, tambourines, basses, and whistles; and when they struck up the *tropak*, the whole house seemed to shake. And Ivan, upon hearing the music, felt even livelier and began to dance around the house. It did not bother him that the *chort* was his guest, or that it was devilish music playing. He danced and danced. Sweat started to drip from him, but he kept on dancing. The *chort* kept pouring *horilka*, drinking himself, and treating the musicians.

"Cock-a-doodle-doo!" crowed the rooster, and all of a sudden, everything disappeared. The *chort* and the music disappeared, leaving Ivan breathless after dancing for so long. He put out the light, collapsed on the bench, and fell into a deep sleep.

It was already late when Ivan got up and began

recounting to his wife about how he had partied, and how the music played, and he danced. His wife listened and was glad that she had fallen asleep and missed the whole affair. Ivan washed up, prayed to God, drank a couple of glasses of *horilka*, ate his breakfast, and then went to the village to buy cattle. He bought all sorts of animals: cows, oxen, horses, sheep, and pigs, and various clothing, He also bought all sorts of clothing, and started living like a proper landowner.

At first, while people still were unaware of how Ivan had obtained his wealth, they visited him and showed respect. But once the rumour spread throughout the village that he had been endowed with money by an unclean spirit, no one wanted anything to do with him. They even told the priest about it, and the priest also distanced himself from Ivan. But Ivan did not care; he had purchased everything he needed, lived comfortably on his own, and believed that the *chort* would eventually forget about his money.

"Tonight, wife, I want to go visiting," Ivan told his wife one evening, "because the nobleman who gave me all that money invited me to his place."

"Go," his wife told him, "but it's already late."

"He told me to come to him at midnight," Ivan replied. "You know, being the *chort* he prefers no other time but midnight. Otherwise, if I don't go to him, he might take the money back."

Ivan waited until it was late at night, when everyone had gone to sleep. He put on his hat and went to the same forest where he had picked the fern flower.

He entered the forest, and after walking just about twenty steps, he saw before him a palace like he had never seen before. And the windows! They were countless! The whole building was blazing with light; it was so bright throughout the house that you could find a needle. Ivan was amazed and began to climb the porch... and what a high porch it was! Ivan climbed and climbed... until he reached the entrance. Opening the door, he stepped inside and saw people everywhere.

"Good health to you, Ivan!" said the host to him. "Thank you for not forgetting about us. Come, sit at the table."

When Ivan looked at the table, it was filled with all sorts of delicacies: roasted piglets, cured meats, and various types of *horilka* – there was even *varenukha* and spicy *horilka*. Ivan sat at the table, drank *horilka*, and ate whatever he could. After dinner, they got up from the table, the music started playing, and they began to dance. No one stood out more than our Ivan – he danced, squatted, and performed all sorts of moves. When they finally stopped dancing, they resumed drinking *horilka* again.

"How is your wife?" asked the host, handing Ivan a glass of *varenukha*.

"She is well, thank God!" Ivan , taking the glass and crossing himself…

That very moment, the palace and all the people disappeared. Ivan looked around: what's the hell? It seemed like there was water beneath him – he looked closer and saw that he was standing on a mill's wheel, holding onto its roof with one hand, with water running beneath his feet. Ivan was terribly frightened to lose his balance and fall into the abyss below, but then he gathered himself and began to slowly climb down from the wheel. Somehow, he reached a

bridge, and stepping onto it, he crossed himself.

"Thank God the mill wasn't running, or I'd be dead," Ivan said. "What tricks the unclean spirits come up with! I came here as a guest, and they tried to kill me. *Tsur you! Pek you!* I will never set foot in this forest again, and you should stay away from me too!"

Saying this, Ivan slowly made his way back to the village, thinking about how he had tricked the *chort* into giving him money and convincing him to take his soul in fifteen years.

Since the time, when instead of showing hospitality to Ivan, the *chorty* nearly drowned him, the cursed *chort* never showed himself to Ivan again.

Years flew by. Ten years passed but the *chort* who gave him the money never showed up again. Ivan did nothing but laugh at the *chort*, proud that he had tricked him. Fourteen years passed, then the fifteenth year began, and Ivan lived in comfort and plenty.

"Today, wife," Ivan said to his wife, "marks exactly fifteen years since the *chort* gave me money, and he still hasn't come for me. That's why we have all this! Even though I used to be a drunkard, look at how much I've acquired! Shows I had brains to trick the *chort* himself! Ha, ha, ha!" Ivan laughed heartily at having outwitted the *chort*."

"Giddy up! Giddy up! Damn you!" Old Okhrymenko shouted at his mare while hauling flour from the mill –his mare had stopped and no matter how much he urged her on, she would not move and just stood there.

"Good health to you!" someone said, approaching Okhrymenko. Okhrymenko turned around and saw a man in a splendid zhupan and hat standing before him.

"Good health to you too!" Okhrymenko replied.

"Why are you standing here with a cart?" the nobleman asked Okhrymenko.

"Well, you see, kind sir," Okhrymenko explained, "I'm hauling this flour from the mill, but my mare has stopped, and won't go any further."

"What are you talking about?" the nobleman said. "She's just being lazy. Come, get on the cart with me, and let's give her a go. You'll see how she'll run!"

"No, sir, there's no way she'd run, we'll have to stay here until morning!" Okhrymenko replied.

"Just listen to me and get on!" the nobleman told Okhrymenko. Okhrymenko climbed onto the cart with the nobleman. He hadn't even settled in yet when the mare, tail raised, suddenly bolted off, as if possessed. Okhrymenko did not need to urge her on; she flew forward on her own, full of energy.

"Thank you, sir," Okhrymenko said to the nobleman, "for advising me on what to do. I thought she was truly exhausted, but it turns out she was just being stubborn. As soon as I got on the cart and showed her the whip, she took off!.."

Soon they reached the village. The nobleman said to Okhrymenko,

"Wait a moment, man! I'll get off the cart here – that's the street I need."

Okhrymenko stopped his mare, and the nobleman got off the cart.

"And where are you headed, sir?" Okhrymenko asked the nobleman.

"I have some business to attend to," the nobleman replied. "I lent some money to a man here, and I'm going to settle accounts with him."

"Which man?" Okhrymenko asked. "I think I know everyone in our village."

"The one who lives next to your deacon's wife," the nobleman said.

"Oh!" Okhrymenko said, "That's Ivan, who used to be a terrible drunkard and had nothing, but now there's hardly anyone in the village who lives as well as he does...

Did you give him the money?" Okhrymenko asked the nobleman. "We've heard all sorts of rumours in the village about..."

At that moment Okhrymenko crossed himself. "You see," he was about to say, "there were rumours that Ivan got his money from the *chort*..." And as soon as he crossed himself because he mentioned *chort* by his name – in an instant, the nobleman who had travelled with him on the cart vanished. It was then that our Okhrymenko realised why his mare had bolted and who had been sitting with him on the cart. He crossed himself again and tried to urge his mare on, but she stood as if rooted to the spot. He struggled with her for a while, then went home to get another horse. When he returned, he found his mare had stiffened. He unharnessed her and harnessed the other horse and travelled home.

The day after what happened to Okhrymenko, word spread throughout the village that although Ivan had been perfectly healthy and had dinner with his wife and children the previous evening, in the morning, his wife found him lying dead on the bench. People also said that a man passing by Ivan's house late at night saw a light inside and glimpsed two men sitting at the table through the window.

But here's the strange part: Ivan's wife, after crying over her husband, went out of the house and checked the sheepfold, only to find all the sheep lying dead on the ground. She rushed to the cowshed, and the cows and horses were dead too. She hurried to her husband's clothes to get the money, but the purse with the chervontsi was already gone. She went to the storeroom, opened the chest – and instead of the *plakhta*, *zapaska*, and various other things they had bought with the money her husband had received, she found only rotten straw. She looked at herself: thinking she was wearing her new, blue *plakhta* and red *zapaska* that she had recently bought at the fair, but instead, she saw the old, tattered clothes she used to wear when they were poor. Everywhere she looked, there was nothing of value: everything had vanished without a trace! The fine clothes her children and husband had worn were gone, and they were left with the old rags they had when they were poor.

Word spread throughout the entire village that Okhrymenko had seen and even given a ride to a certain nobleman, who told him he was going to Ivan's place to settle a debt, as he had lent Ivan money. Everyone quickly realised that Ivan had prospered with the *chort's* help.

But what good did it do him? His wife and children, who had once been destitute, were now left in the same state, and all the livestock he had acquired was gone in an instant. People pitied Ivan's wife and his poor children, especially since their neighbour, who used to feed them and wanted to take them in as his own, had long passed away, leaving his wealth to the church, and there was nothing left for them to do but return to begging. And whenever anyone recalled Ivan's story, they would say, "Easy come, easy go."

Endnotes

[11] *Ivan Kupalo Night* – the original uses "tonight"; see definition of *Ivan Kupalo Night* in the Glossary.

No, You Won't Escape: You've Crossed Paths with the Wrong Person!

In the village of T..., an old woman named Priska shared a story with me when I asked her for a fairy tale.

***

"But this isn't a fairy tale; it actually happened. People tell, there once lived a very wealthy Pan in this village who had a young wife. He was quite old, while she was still young; he loved his wife dearly, but she didn't return his affection – after all, who would love such an old man? Their time together was brief: the Pan, being old, soon passed away, leaving her a widow. What happened then? Villagers said he was a very powerful warlock, and, after his death, he decided to visit his wife.

"Here's what happened! Right after they buried him and finished the funeral meal, in the evening, his widow went to their small cottage where they used to share a bed. She mourned there briefly before laying down and falling asleep. I don't know how long she slept, but suddenly, she felt someone waking her up. She opened her eyes... And what do you think? Standing before her was her husband, whom she had just buried, and beside the bed, on the floor, was a coffin; and one of his feet was inside the coffin, and the other on the floor. She was terrified and wanted to scream for help, but the revenant gestured with his hand for her to be silent. She had no choice but to keep silent! The door of the cottage was locked. Then the revenant stepped out of the coffin, sat on the bed beside his wife, and began to

110

kiss and caress her as if he were a living man. Although the woman was afraid of him, what could she do? All he ever knew was how to drink like a fish, and he did just that. Then, as the rooster was about to crow, he said to his wife:

"Look here, wife! By tomorrow, you must cook all sorts of things – because tomorrow I shall have guests with me, and there should be plenty to eat and drink.

With these words, he kissed her and lay back in the coffin again. All of a sudden, as though a gust of wind had passed, the door swung open and four ghosts, each adorned with horns and hook-like tails, appeared. They lifted the coffin and bore it out of the dwelling and all fell silent, except for the sound of something with wheels rattling

across the courtyard. She made the sign of the cross and summoned her maid. Soon, the maid entered. She inquired whether the maid had heard or seen any strange events. The maid recounted that she and the other maids were in the kitchen and heard someone nearing the cottage; through the doors, they saw the coffin being carried and brought into the Pan's house.

Terrified of being alone overnight, the Pani implored her maid to stay with her in the house. Waking up the next morning, she was consumed by melancholy. She was told that the estate workers had witnessed a carriage drawn by four black horses arriving in the courtyard, stopping right beside the house, where four men unloaded a coffin and carried it into the manor.

She dreaded the night as though it were her own end, bracing for the revenant's return. As dusk fell, the Pani summoned numerous people, seeking their company overnight at her residence in hopes that their presence might deter the revenant from visiting. Night fell, and as it grew later, she stayed vigilant, the thought of sleep didn't even cross her mind.

Nobody slept; there were perhaps a dozen people in the Pani's house. And again, they heard footsteps approaching the manor, and again the door swung open as though pushed by the wind. And again, the same ghosts who had appeared before carried the coffin inside the Pani's house...

And oh, I forgot to mention," the old woman recounted, "the Pani had prepared *horilka*, meat dishes, and set the table, as the revenant had instructed. The ghosts brought the coffin into the room, placed it beside the bed, and then went into the main hall, which became so crowded with unclean spirits that there was barely room to drop a needle.

The coffin lid flew open, and the revenant arose. The sight of the revenant, who was none other than their recently interred lord, petrified everyone. The revenant looked around, his eyes glowing like fiery embers and foam frothing at his mouth. He gestured for everyone to leave the room. Though they felt sympathy for their lady, they had no choice but to hurriedly exit. As they left the house,

the revenant once again sat on the bed and began kissing and caressing his wife.

And what was happening in the main hall?

The Pani's bed was placed directly opposite the door to the main hall, and she could see a remarkable number of *chorty* had gathered; they sat down at the table, feasting and indulging in *horilka*. After they drained every last drop, they began to dance, with music mysteriously emerging from nowhere. Then the time came once again for the revenant to return to his resting place, and again, after kissing his wife goodbye, he lay back into the coffin and was carried out of the house. In her fright, the Pani summoned others for comfort, staying awake until the break of dawn. Only in the early morning did she manage to fall asleep. Upon waking, she contemplated how to ensure the revenant would not return. At that time, a traveller was passing through the village; having arrived late the previous night. The Pani approached him to seek help in banishing the revenant, recounting to him the eerie visits of her recently deceased husband over the past two nights, each time arriving in a carriage drawn by four horses.

They waited until nightfall, and A. summoned the village folk, leading them to the bridge. Before they could reach it, they heard the rumble of wheels so thunderous it seemed the earth itself quaked. Suspecting the revenant's approach, A. instructed the townsfolk to remain near the bridge – a crowd would repel the revenant, but he alone might go unnoticed. Bravely, he advanced towards the bridge.

As he set foot on the bridge, he saw a carriage drawn by four horses hurtling toward him. He walked forward, and as the horses reached him, both they and the carriage vanished beneath the bridge with a deafening roar, leaving only a coffin behind. A. beckoned to the villagers, showed them the coffin, and instructed them to return at dawn to impale the revenant with an aspen stake.

"And now," he declared, "let him remain on the bridge until morning – for it is too late for him to escape us."

After saying this, A. returned home, and the villagers dispersed to their homes. At dawn, they gathered again, went to the bridge, and found the coffin. They dug a grave nearby and impaled the revenant with a stake. From that day forward, the revenant ceased to appear to the Pani, who had once been his wife.

"That's what happened in this village!" the old woman told me. "And don't think it's just a fib – no! It's true, indeed it's true!"

The end

Index

Glossary

A postcard entitled 'Portrait of S. Yashnyi, a Kobzar' by Slastion, 1903, featuring a bandura player.

Life style and Traditions

Bandura (plural: *bandury*): is a traditional Ukrainian stringed musical instrument. It has a large, rounded body with a short neck and typically features a combination of 12 to 68 strings. The instrument is played by plucking the strings with the fingers of both hands.

The *bandura* is deeply rooted in Ukrainian culture and history, often associated with the *kobzari* or *bandurysty*, itinerant blind musicians who played the *bandura* and sang epic poems called *dumy* about historical events and heroic figures. The instrument has a distinctive, harp-like sound and is used in both folk and classical music settings.

In recent times, the *bandura* has seen a resurgence in popularity and is recognised as a symbol of Ukrainian national identity and cultural heritage.

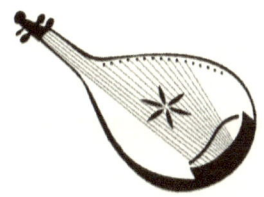

*C*hort (plural: *chorty*): A *chort* is a mythological evil spirit in Ukrainian folklore, typically depicted as a male figure. These spirits have the ability to change their appearance, transforming into a man or an animal.

Often, a *chort* is portrayed as a man with small horns, fur, a tail, and hooves. Despite their fearsome attributes, *chorty* can be killed.

Chorty primarily reside in hell, but on earth, they are believed to inhabit deserted places, crossroads, and other eerie locations. These spirits possess magical powers, which they predominantly use at night. Their main objective is to cause harm to humans, often by leading them into evil deeds and misfortune.

"And the musicians pounded themselves on the cheeks with their fists, as if on tambourines, and hummed through their noses as if playing Frenchwuw horns...", illustration by I. Prianishnikov (1874-76) from M. Hohol's novel The Lost Letter; *featuring chorty.*

*C*humak (plural: *chumaky*): Ukrainian ox-cart drivers and traders who engaged in long-distance trade during the 15th to 19th centuries. *Chumaky* primarily transported salt, fish, grain, and other goods across vast distances, often travelling to the Black Sea and Crimean regions. The life of a *chumak* was arduous and required resilience, as they often faced difficult travelling conditions and threats from bandits. For that reason, *chumaky* were admired by the Ukrainian people for their bravery and are often mentioned in folklore.

"Chumak on the road; Farmer from the vicinity of Uman" by Jan Nepomucen Lewicki (1841).

124

Fern flower: Also known as "Perun's flower" in Slavic mythology, is a mythical blossom said to appear only once a year on the night of *Ivan Kupalo* (*Kupala* Night), which coincides with the summer solstice. It is believed to possess magical properties and is associated with hidden treasures. See also *Ivan Kupalo Night*.

"'Now it's time', thought Petro and reached out his hand." by Borzh, in M. Hohol's The Night of Ivan Kupala, *1902).*

*I*van Kupalo Night: Also known as *Kupala* Night, is a traditional Slavic holiday celebrated in Ukraine, Poland, and some other countries, marking the summer solstice. The festival is associated with ancient pagan rituals and is held on the night of July 6th to 7th.

A central element of the festivities is the lighting of large bonfires. Participants, especially young couples, jump over these fires as a test of bravery and a ritual for purification and fertility. It is believed that those couples who successfully

leap over the flames together will have a prosperous and happy future.

Girls weave and wear wreaths of field flowers. They then float these wreaths on rivers or streams, interpreting their movement to predict their romantic futures.

Water plays a significant role in the celebration. People engage in various water-related activities, including swimming and splashing, symbolising purification and the healing powers of nature.

A key mythical aspect of *Ivan Kupalo Night* is the search for the elusive and magical fern flower, which is said to bloom only on this night. Finding it is believed to grant the seeker prosperity, luck, and the ability to understand the language of animals.

"Girls Divining on the Night of Ivan Kupalo"
by Ivan Sokolov (1856).

Klechalna Sunday: This focal day of *Zeleni Sviata* (Engl., 'Green Holidays') in Christianity, holiday is known as Pentecost, the date of which varies annually and occurs 50 days after Easter Sunday. It is a significant day in Ukrainian religious and cultural life, blending Christian and ancient folk traditions.

Zeleni Sviata is an ancient multi-day celebration associated with the cult of the Sun, nature, and ancestors. In Ukrainian mythology, this is the time when *rusalky* are most active.

With some variations across Ukraine, *Zeleni Sviata* begins on *Klechalna* Saturday, the day before Pentecost (Sunday), and ends with the last three days of *Zelenyi Tyzhden* (Trinity Week).

'*Trinity Eve in Ukraine*' *by M. Tkachenko,* in Vsemirnaya Illiustratsiya
(1898, no. 22).

Otaman (plural: otamany): A term historically used in Ukrainian and *kozak* contexts to denote a military leader or commander. "Otaman" is also used more generally to denote a leader or chief.

Pan (plural: pany): In Ukrainian, "Pan" is a term of respect used to address a man. It is equivalent to "Mr." in English and is often used in formal or polite conversation. The term is a holdover from historical times and can convey a sense of respect, politeness, and sometimes social status.

Pereliak (plural: *pereliaky*): This is a personified disease, caused by a scare, which may lead to death.

To find out what scared the person and caused *pereliak*, a *znakharka* (traditional folk healer) rolled an egg over the patient's body while reading prayers. Then they broke the eggshell and poured the egg white into a glass half-filled with water and looking into the glass with the light behind they tried to guess the reason for *pereliak*. The water with the egg white afterwards was given to a dog.

*P*ich (plural: *pechi*): This brick, clay, or tile structure served multiple functions in a traditional Ukrainian house: it was used for heating and cooking, and some designs included an area where one could sit or lie. The cult of the *pich*, as an extension of the cult of fire and the sun, is manifested in many aspects of Ukrainian culture. The folk's respect for the *pich* is evident from an old Ukrainian saying, "I would say [something improper], but there is a *pich* in the house".

'The Mistress of the House by the Pich' by Mykhaltseva (in Sketches from Travels across Ukraine, 1882, p. 13).

'Svaty' by Mykola Pymonenko (1882). The image includes the following elements defined in the glossary: pich, pokuttia, starosty, ochipok, plakhta, sorochka, svyta, and zapaska.

*P*okuttia: The special corner in the main room of an old-style traditional Ukrainian house, where the icons are placed, is called the pokuttia.

The *pokuttia* was considered to be an honourable place. At Christmas a family placed *didukh* (a ritual sheaf of ears), *kutia* and *uzvar* (dishes) in that corner.

Detail of: 'Epiphany Eve' by M. Tkachenko, Zhivopisnoe Obozrenie no. 2 (1895); featuring pokuttia with icons adorned with rushnyky.

*R*usalka (plural: *rusalky*): A mythological female figure, the *rusalka* shares some characteristics with mermaids and sirens but has a very distinct nature that was developed through centuries of Ukrainian mythology.

Rusalky are the souls of young women, who have died an unnatural death, such as drowning or suicide. They prefer to live in standing water – ponds or rivers that are still or have a slow-moving current. Usually, they come out from the water in the warm months during the new moon. They are dressed in long, delicate white *sorochky* or are naked.

Rusalky are mischievous and, as a game, give riddles to a passer-by, and if the latter does not give the correct answer, *rusalky* kill them. They tickle them to death and drag their bodies under the water. It is advisable to avoid places popular with *rusalky* at the time when they are most active, but if one had to go there, they should carry some wormwood with them as an amulet to ward off the beautiful wicked spirits.

'Rusalky' by Taras Shevchenko (c. 1859–1860).

'Kozak' by Amvrosiy Zhdakha (1912), a Chas Publishing House postcard, Kyiv.

*S*tarosta (plural: *starosty*): In a traditional Ukrainian wedding, *starosty* are honoured elders or respected individuals chosen to act as intermediaries and representatives of the bride and groom's families. They play a significant role in the matchmaking and engagement process (see definition of *svataty*). During the wedding ceremony, the *starosty* also lead certain rituals.

*T*ropak: A traditional Ukrainian folk dance characterised by its fast tempo and lively, energetic movements. The *tropak* is performed in 2/4 time. It features a series of rapid steps, jumps, and spins. It is often accompanied by traditional Ukrainian music played on instruments such as the *bandura*, *sopilka* (cf. flute), or violin. The dance is popular at celebrations and festivals.

*T*sur you! Pek you: The phrase is a Ukrainian expression used to ward off or reject something undesirable or to express strong disapproval. It roughly translates to "To hell with you!" or "Away with you!" in English. Thus, this is an emphatic way of saying that something should be cast away or sent to hell.

Fashion

Ochipok (plural: *ochipky*): This obsolete Ukrainian women's headwear, a type of hat, was traditionally worn by married women. It often has a slit at the back, which is laced up to hold the hair hidden underneath.

'Various kinds of ochipok', in Vovk's Studies on Ukrainian Ethnography and Anthropology *1928, Table 11).*

Plakhta (plural: *plakhty*): A traditional Ukrainian women's garment, similar to a skirt, made from woven fabric. The *plakhta* consists of two rectangular pieces of cloth wrapped around the waist and secured with a belt. It is often made from brightly coloured, patterned wool or cotton, featuring intricate geometric designs. The *plakhta* is typically worn over *sorochka* and is an essential part of traditional Ukrainian folk attire.

'Festive attire, Ternopil region, 1932', a page from O. Kulchytska's album Folk Clothing of the Western Regions of the Ukrainian SSR, *1959, Table 11).*

'A Noble Maiden' by Tymofiy Kalynskyi (1847).

'A Village Girl' by Tymofiy Kalynskyi (1847).

*S*orochka (plural: *sorochky*): (1) An old-fashioned light, loose undergarment, a type of long shirt with sleeves; and (2) an upper garment, a type of blouse with sleeves. The *sorochka* is an essential part of Ukrainian folk attire. The embroidery patterns on a *sorochka* vary by region.

'After Bathing' by K. Trutovskyi (1890); featuring a girl in sorochka.

144

Svyta (plural: *svyty*): A traditional Ukrainian outer garment, typically made from homespun coarse woollen cloth. The *svyta* is a long, loose-fitting coat or cloak worn by both men and women. It often features intricate embroidery and decorative elements, reflecting regional styles.

Yupka (plural: *yupky*): This old-fashioned traditional outer garment, a type of long jacket, is buttoned up at the front, and is typically worn over a blouse or dress.

Zapaska (plural: *zapasky*): is a traditional Ukrainian garment worn by women. It is a type of wrap-around skirt or apron that is part of traditional folk dress. The *zapaska* is typically made from a rectangular piece of cloth and can be either open at the sides or completely wrapped around the waist.

Zhupan (plural: *zhupany*): A traditional, now obsolete, long outerwear garment worn by both men and women in Ukraine. The *zhupan* was popular among Ukrainian *kozaky* and became a distinctive element of their cultural and military dress. Typically, *zhupany* were made of rich fabrics and adorned with intricate embroidery, reflecting the wearer's status.

Cuisine

Borshch (plural: *borshchi*): Also, borsch; this traditional Ukrainian dish has beetroot as its main ingredient. Other ingredients may include: cabbage, potatoes, tomatoes, meat and fish. *Borshch* is one of several traditional dishes most often mentioned in the native folklore.

Horilka: Derived from the verb hority, 'to burn', *horilka* is a strong Ukrainian distilled spirit.

Kovbasa: This traditional Ukrainian sausage is made from ground meat, usually pork, although beef, chicken, or a mixture of meats can also be used. The meat is typically seasoned with garlic, salt, pepper, and other spices before being stuffed into a natural or synthetic casing. *Kovbasa* is known for its rich, savoury flavour and can be smoked, dried, or cooked fresh.

Pampushky (singular: *pampushka*): Traditional Ukrainian yeast-raised buns or doughnuts that are typically served as a side dish or dessert. They come in both sweet and savoury varieties and hold a special place in Ukrainian cuisine.

*S*alo (mass noun): A traditional Ukrainian dish consisting of slabs of cured pork (salted, brine-fermented, or smoked). *Salo* is traditionally served as part of a sandwich but may also be fried to make 'shkvarky' (cracklings), which can be added to soups or used as a dressing for other traditional Ukrainian dishes.

Detail of: 'At Godfather's on New Year's Eve' by M. Tkachenko, in Vsemirnaya Illiustratsiya (1898); featuring various dishes including a ring of kovbasa.

Varenukha: A traditional Ukrainian beverage that can have either no alcohol or a low percentage of alcohol. The alcoholic version of the drink consists of *horilka* cooked with honey, dried fruit, and spices. The non-alcoholic version is made with dried fruit cooked in water, honey, herbs, and spices.

Varenukha was popular until the beginning of the 20th century and was made for special family occasions and religious holidays. This drink was also popular among the *kozaky*, who strictly prohibited alcohol during their military campaigns but enjoyed a good *varenukha* during their repose.

'Guest from Zaporizhzhia' by Fotiy Krasytskyi (1916).

sova
BOOKS

Sova Books Publications

Fiction

Gabor, Vasyl 2024, *A Book of Exotic Dreams and Real Events*

Polishchuk, Klym 2015, *Treasure of the Ages. Ukrainian Legends*

Sacher-Masoch, Leopold von and Haivoronskyi, Petro 2016, *Bloody Wedding in Kyiv: Two Tales of Olha, Kniahynia of Kyivan Rus*

Skovoroda, Hryhoriy 2022, *Aphorisms by Skovoroda: Ukrainian Explorations of Love and Life*

Soldatova, Svitlana (ill.) 2018, *The Mitten* (Colouring Book)

Soldatova, Svitlana (ill.) 2018, *The Sparrow and the Bush & The Little Straw Bull* (Colouring Book)

Somov, Orest 2016, *The Witches of Kyiv and Other Gothic Tales*

Starytska-Cherniakhivska, Liudmyla 2015, The Living Grave

Storozhenko, Oleksa 2024, *Marko the Damned*

Yohansen, Mike 2021, *The Journey of the Learned Doctor Leonardo and his Future Lover, the Beauteous Alceste, to the Switzerland of Slobozhanshchyna*

Non-fiction

Myloradovych, Vasyl 2021, *Notes on Ukrainian Demonology*

Sumtsov, Mykola & ors 2019, *The Story of Pysanka: A Collection of Articles on Ukrainian Easter Eggs*

Yakovenko, Svitlana 2016, *Ukrainian Christmas Eve Supper: Traditional Village Recipes for Sviata Vecheria*

Yakovenko, Svitlana 2017, *Ancient Grains: Ukrainian Recipes*

Yakovenko, Svitlana 2017, *Traditional Velykden: Ukrainian Easter Recipes*

Yefymenko, Petro 2020, *A Collection of Ukrainian Spells*